Advocate of Time
By
Craig Allan

© 2014, Craig Allan

ISBN: 978-0-9903031-1-4

Advocate of Time
By
Craig Allan

Craig Allan
Advocate of Time

© 2014, Craig Allan

Special Thanks to

I would like to thank everyone who put effort and time into me as I allowed The Holy Spirit to move through me over time to create this book. It is part of my life's work finally come to fruition.

I wish to thank my great kids for reading this book and giving me some positive feedback about what they thought of the story.

I thank my wife for her sacrifice of time spent with me while I worked on this book and other research projects. She has been an inspiration to me and I love her for standing by me through all of this. I love you Baby!

Thanks to my Mom who believed all along I could do it, even though she knew I had many distractions along the way.

Special thanks to Andrew and Judit Raduly for their help in this project.

Thanks to Andrew Raduly Photography for the photo used as the cover.

A special thanks to Free from Evil Spirits Ministries and Buffy Olson, who has grown right along with me in this publication process. It has taken us some time, some re-writes and some long changes, but we made it. Now on to our next chapter, let our Great God shine through all we do!

And most of all, Thank you Jesus my Savior, my friend, my brother and my Lord for giving me the inspiration, strength and heart to see this project through to the end. I look forward to more to come.

Praise Him!

Blessings,

Craig Allan

This Book is dedicated to

This biblically inspired work is dedicated to my loving family who stood by me through the long days and nights I was unavailable while I was writing.

To my loving and supportive wife Tanya who graciously made time for me to work and kept our home functioning, and most of all to my Lord and Savior Jesus Christ who inspired me with His Holy Spirit, His words and the support I needed to pick up my cross and carry on.

Contents

THE ADVOCATE OF TIME   Webster   Craig Allan

Chapter 1

Webster

Aganon, the angel of time, descends out of the clouds in full glory with a shroud of light causing his angelic body to shine in likeness to a bright star.

His wings are outstretched in descent and his clothing is a wave of motion like liquid; bright and shining, glowing with a luminescence that is not mistaken for anything less than heavenly glory. His robes flow like a river crashing along a rocky shore. The robe covering his upper body is a silvery color with slight traces of gold flowing throughout. Aganon's waistband is a braided golden rope that appears to be softer than any fabric imagined and the ends of the rope flow out behind him below his fluttering wings. The rope snaps and pops in the crashing wind that envelopes him. The robe covering his lower body is darker in contrast to his upper robes as it flows with highlights of the faintest teal and aquamarine. It flashes and wavers around his amber, glowing legs. His bare feet lay out behind him as he continues his approach to earth. He dims his radiance as he comes into sight of the town of Webster.

Aganon's thoughts return to his charge, "Here, the town of Webster, where I'll find my charge, to take the chosen ones on their journey for enlightenment and wisdom. Oh Lord, have they any idea of the thing that they ask?"

The rooftops of the houses are just below his reach as he comes to rest on the roof of the Webster Seventh Day Adventist Church. As he alights on the crest of the roof, he can feel the power of the prayers of his charge.

"They have excellent prayer work to The Lord. They shall surely do well." He says to the night.

"Yes, they certainly will, provided they keep His commandments." Percival, the angel of the watch, answers as he steps out from the steeple.

"His glory, His name," Aganon greets Percival.

"His name, His glory," Percival returns the greeting.

"Do you think they know how important their prayer work is Percy?" Aganon asks.

"Of course they do Ag, why else would you be here?"

Aganon nods in agreement.

"Do they attend His presence in this house of God often Percy?" Aganon asks.

"They are here no less than three days each week, are you wondering if their faith is adequate for such a charge as yours?" Percival replies.

"No, I do not question their faith. I am challenging their commitment to it," Aganon replies.

"Aganon, taking six young believers traveling through time to see the great works of God is no small thing." Percival says, resting his hand on Aganon's shoulder.

"The Lord God would not entrust such a task to anyone but you, and to no human less than worthy of the charge. Our Maker is aware of the risks, yet it is what they have requested. They all desire this quest; and their faith is great. I myself have heard their prayers" Percival pauses, "I have even felt them, for several years now."

He pauses again, "they are ready."

"Yes, I know of their reverent desire for enlightenment and better understanding of His word and His will," Aganon replies. "I am just not certain they are prepared for the way in which their enlightenment will come. It seems like such a large step in a short time."

Aganon ponders those thoughts for a few moments while looking out over the Webster night. Finally Aganon squats down and asks,

"Ok Percy, where are they? I know they are close, I can feel them."

"They are at Webster's Study Inn," Percival says pointing toward town, "a small diner just up the street. It is where they meet to pray, study God's Word, and hang out. You will love it, the establishment is a portrayal of a library, there are bookshelves with hundreds of books, the tables have reading lights, and when they bring your food they take the books back so you can eat. Some real creative works went into the design of such a place."

"Sounds like the perfect place to meet," Aganon replied, "time to get into character. Thanks for receiving me, Percy," he says, thrusting his hand out toward Percival for a farewell handshake. Percival raises one eyebrow in wonder then laughs and take Aganon's hand and shakes it vigorously.

"I like your character already, Ag," Percival chuckles. "God's speed to you my friend, may your charge be blessed by His grace and love."

Percival sets his hand on Aganon's shoulder in a farewell gesture and nods approvingly. Aganon nods back, turns, and steps off the roof. As he descends to the ground, twenty-five feet below, his wings flutter behind him and transform into a long overcoat. His brilliant golden robes fade and begin to change into a button down western shirt with faded blue jeans, his braided waist belt is now a leather belt. Aganon's long flowing hair is transformed into a wide brimmed black cowboy hat. Under his right arm a coiled bullwhips appears and under his left arm a rolled lariat rope. He lands in a squat on the lawn in the back yard of the church. The moment his amber shinning feet touch the grass his bare feet are adorned in a shiny black pair of cowboy boots.

Aganon stands, looks up at Percival, and grins. Percival motions as if he is tipping his hat then waves. Aganon tips his hat.

Aganon sets out toward the Webster Study Inn to meet his charge and get to know the six kids he will come to know as disciples of the Most High. Aganon strides down the street toward the Webster Study Inn. He is playing the part of a rambling cowpoke looking for work, and no trouble. As he looks around the city of Webster in the relaxing quiet of summer cool, he understands why his charge has adorned him the garments he wears. Webster is a mid-sized southwestern cattle town with a train rail and a highway passing through. There is desert to the south and mountains to the north. He looks like any other cowpoke rambler looking for work on his way to somewhere else.

As Aganon comes into sight of the Webster study inn, he sees the spiritual battle that follows these children of God everywhere they go. The angels of God fight off the demons that attempt to reach these Godly kids. The demons are no match for the angelic watchmen whose charge is to safeguard each of the faithful. The prayer power is so strong that the angelic defenses cannot be penetrated. Yet, the forces of darkness are relentless. Aganon approaches the entrance to the diner. The watchmen; six all together, gather together and drop to one knee in what appears to be an act of reverence. Aganon stops and watches the demons pounce on these warrior watchmen as they kneel in honor and respect of their time traveling brother. As the dark spirits continue to pile upon the watchmen, they become engulfed in the flood of foul dark forces. Aganon prepares to leap into battle to defend his brothers, when he hears the battle cries of glory pulsating from within the writhing mound of demons. In a brilliant flash of light and song that vaporizes the evil forces that surrounded them, the six watchmen stand from their kneeling position with their swords thrust toward the heavens. As the few remaining demonic forces flee the area, the watchmen sheath their swords and nod in greeting to Aganon, the angel of time. Aganon nods, returning the greeting. The watchmen return to their posts to safeguard their faithful.

Aganon turns toward the diner and walks to the door. He reaches forward to grasp the handle to go inside, and pauses for a moment. He gathers another few moments of power from the prayer coverage, checks his mental notes, opens the door, and goes inside.

The inside of the diner is exactly as Percy described it. The walls of this small eating establishment are completely covered with hundreds of volumes of books. Everywhere he looks is a bookshelf full of books; even the tables where the customers sit have bookshelves against the wall with a few volumes on them. This establishment is a hungry scholar's dream come true.

Aganon walks up the counter and sits down on a high back chair that even looks the part of a scholarly establishment. Aganon settles in to his chair and begins to slowly look around the diner.

There is a rancher sitting at the other end of the counter sipping coffee and looking at the paper. Behind him to his right, a family of four is having a late dinner. Off to his right, the diner opens up into a larger room with a few tables situated in the center of the room. The walls are lined with bookshelves filled with books. Sitting at the table in the very center of the room are six high school kids. They are reading from the bible and discussing the scriptures. One of them is keeping a journal, writing down the thoughts of the group. This is his charge. Here are the six young people who will become an important part of his days and weeks to come. He looks away and takes the menu from the counter to turn his attention elsewhere. It would not do him well to start off his meeting with them by staring at them like zoo animals. A waitress steps up to him while he is looking at the menu and gathering his thoughts.

"Howdy there cowboy, you're new around here," the waitress says.

"Yes ma'am, just passing through and looking for some work," Aganon replies. This cowpoke role comes naturally, Aganon considers.

"Can I get you anything?" she asks, looking him over a bit as something unknown lingers about this stranger. The waitress cannot recognize the heavenly presence that surrounds him.

Aganon's voice interrupts her thoughts "Yes ma'am, coffee please."

"Coming right up," She says as she turns toward the coffee pot, still unsure about the odd presence of the traveling cowpoke. She fumbles with the coffee, continually glancing toward Aganon trying to piece together what is so different about him. As she brings his coffee Aganon smiles at her in a warm and comforting way, driving away her fears and doubts. The warmth of the benevolence flowing from him calms her and a peace fills her spirit. She goes about her business, and then smiling in peace and joy she enjoys the best day she's had in years.

Aganon grasps the cup of coffee between his hands and looks at the dark liquid in the cup.

"The time is now," echoes in his conscious thoughts.

Aganon gets up with his cup of coffee and strides into the study room. In the study room he sets his cup down at a table next to the kids and goes to the bookshelves to have a look. Finding a hardcover book of biblical history and geography, he takes it back to his table and sets it down. Aganon sits down at the table facing the kids so they can see the book he is reading. He picks up the coffee and takes a sip. Even though the liquid goes into his mouth and disappears there, he can still taste the robust flavor of coffee beans with the tiny taste of municipal water and even the taste of sediment in the water supply of the city.

He picks up the book and opens it to the section where Moses is introduced as a baby and is sent into the river by his mother to save his life. Aganon notices many inaccuracies in the book, but he understands the human desire to reach an understanding of the times of old, and their need to fill in the blanks with their own ideas of what may have happened. Aganon can feel them watching him, thinking about him. He continues to look over the book, and waits for the right moment to make his move.

Eddie notices the cowboy come into the diner, but does not let it disrupt the flow of the spirit in their study time. He continually glances up at the cowboy as they study the book of Exodus, the story of Moses. He cannot get the idea out of his head that he knows this guy. Eddie thinks that he has seen him before, but cannot remember where or when. He looks around at his friends to see if any of them have noticed the stranger at the table next to them. Joey seems to be the only one who has even looked at him. Joey keeps looking at this guy, and then looks away. Something is up. Eddie feels a sense of urgency all of a sudden.

Eddie has felt responsible for all of his friends ever since he met them at summer camp three years ago. One at a time they all found each other as friends and their six way friendship has continued to grow in

Christ. They are closer than friends, closer than brothers and sisters. Eddie has been like a big brother to them since the time they met and now he feels responsible to make sure he can keep their studies and their journey focused on Jesus Christ and their direction toward God.

Joseph notices the tall cowboy sitting at the table next to them; take a drink of his coffee, he closes his eyes as if meditating on it, then set the cup down. Joseph watches as closely as he can out of the corner of his eye. He does not want to stare, but something is a little off about the way this guy is drinking his coffee. He cannot figure out what it is, but something is odd. He sees him take another drink, then another, all the time keeping his attention on his friends as well. The waitress comes into the study.

"Hey guys, you need anything before I go?" Bev asks, "My shifts about over."

They stare at her in shock. "What's wrong?" Bev asks in earnest.

"Bev," Becky says with a grin, "you never ask us what we need before you leave, never in all the years we've been coming here. Don't get me wrong, we like it. It's just that we always figured you didn't like us being here," she pauses, "you ok?"

Advocate of Time   Craig Allan

"You know," Bev says, "I never did like you being here taking up the tables. But suddenly I feel completely different about a lot of things. Will you guys pray for me and my family too?"

They all look on, dumb-founded at the conversation taking place. "Sure we will Bev," Eddie interjects, "anything in particular?"

"Just for our health and healing and peace for my husband," she replies.

"You bet," Eddie answers, writing down her prayer request on his notepad.

"So do you need anything else then?" She asks again. There is a moment of pause.

"Nah, I guess we're good, Bev, thanks though," Eddie says.

"Ok, have a good one. See ya next Wednesday night," she says. She walks over to Aganon's table, tops off his coffee cup, and then leaves the room.

They continue staring at her as she goes. Finally Robbie breaks the silence saying, "What was that all about?"

"Who knows, she sure seems like she's on cloud nine all of a sudden," Becky replies.

"Maybe she found God's grace," Laura suggests.

"Sure looks that way, let's continue to pray for her," Eddie says.

"Yeah," Angela says, "I hope it lasts."

"Amen," they say in stereo and then they burst out laughing.

While all this is going on, Joseph is still watching the cowboy drink his coffee and read his book. Something is so strange about how he is drinking his coffee, but he still can't figure out what it is. Then, like a flash, it hits him. Joseph has not seen this guy swallow his sips of coffee one time. He has gone through at least two cups of coffee now, large cups, and he has not once swallowed what he has put in his mouth, Joseph is certain of it. He watches for awhile longer, and sure enough, he is not swallowing. The coffee goes in, but does not go down.

"That's impossible," Joseph thinks, "He must be drinking it back in a different way."

Aganon breaks the ice. He pushes his coffee cup away and picks up the book. He turns it toward his charge, and asks, "Do any of you feel the same way I do about the lack of biblical and historical facts in this book?"

Advocate of Time   Craig Allan

They stare at him in silence; Aganon holds the stare.

Chapter 2

The Study Inn

They stare each other down for a full minute. Aganon is holding up the book showing a picture of Moses being picked out of the water by a young woman. She is in a tunnel made of brick and stone that looks to be some sort of under city water way.

"This here historical book says that Moses was found in the water by the wife of Pharaoh," he says, pointing to a paragraph describing the picture, "and that he became a son of the ruler of Egypt." Aganon sets the book down on the table. "Do any of you agree with this alleged historical fact?" he asks.

There is a long moment of silence while they stare at the man at the table next to them. Then Eddie speaks up, breaking the silence.

"Well sir, there are many interpretations of the bible and the stories told in the time of the prophets of God."

"Yes there are young man," Aganon replies, "but what I am asking, is do you agree with this interpretation of the facts?" he asks, pointing at the book in front of him, "Do you believe that Moses was adopted by the Pharaoh's wife and was raised as a son of the ruler of Egypt? That is what the movies and the fairytale stories of this age would have us believe."

Eddie stares at the book for a moment, then turns to look at his bible open on the table to the book of Exodus. They have been studying that exact part of the book of Exodus. Eddie turns back to Aganon and finds his kind face waiting his reply.

"No sir," Eddie finally replies, "I do not accept those stories as factual interpretations of the truth; they are merely stories, and inaccurate at that."

"Do you all agree with this young man?" Aganon asks the group.

They all nod in agreement. Aganon nods in return, closes the book, and sets it on the table.

He stands up, takes his hat off and sets it gently on the book. He turns to the group and says, "I prefer the Word of God which speaks of the way, the truth, and the life."

As they continue to watch and listen, Aganon picks up his hat, and where the historical book was, now lays Eddie's bible, open to the same passage of Exodus describing Moses' adoption. Eddie turns back and looks where his bible was open in front of him.

It's not there. He looks at the bookshelf where the book was taken from, and there is the book, as though it was never taken.

Aganon holds his hat outward to the side, gently bows his head toward them and introduces himself.

"My charge, my name is Aganon. I am a servant of the Most High, an advocate of time. I have come to show to you the things which you so desire; enlightenment and clarity of the scriptures in the purest form."

Eddie stares, dumbfounded at the cowboy standing in front of him, slowly, he gets up from his seat, not turning away from the man in front of him and stands facing him. The others do the same. They all stand facing this man standing before them, claiming to be an angel of the Lord.

"Uh, mister, this is kinda freaking us out. Can I have my bible back please?" Eddie stammers.

"Of course Eddie, I did not take it from you; I only used it to replace a lie with the truth," Aganon replies. He reaches down, picks up the bible and holds it out to Eddie.

Aganon stands holding his hat out to his left side, and Eddie's bible out in front of him.

"Uh, this is a bit odd, don't you think. Why don't we sit down and sort this out?" Eddie says, his voice trembling a bit.

"No way, Eddie, let's get out of here!" Joseph blurts.

"Just a minute," Eddie says holding his hand out toward Joey, "let's just see what he has to say before we fly off the handle."

"Eddie, I watched that guy drink two cups of coffee without swallowing a single drop," Joey says, pointing at Aganon with a trembling hand.

"That's impossible, Joey," Eddie replies, "You just could not see him swallowing from where you were sitting."

"Oh yes I could, and he was not drinking that coffee, it was going into his mouth, and just going somewhere else. But not down his throat," Joey stammers.

"I'm getting scared Eddie," Laura says.

Aganon lowers his hands and quotes from the bible he holds, "For God has not given us a spirit of fear, but of power and of love and of a sound mind."

"2 Timothy, chapter 1, verse 7," Becky confirms.

Aganon nods, "yes Rebecca."

Advocate of Time   Craig Allan

"How do you know her name?" Robbie asks.

Aganon stands where he is and looks from one of
them to the other without saying a word.

Eddie watches him intently. He thinks his eyes look
like puddles of kindness and love; his face, a sea of
calm and hope. Eddie feels at peace with this guy,
when he should be terrified, he wonders why.

Aganon stands his ground, waiting for them to take
in what they have seen and heard.

Eddie breaks the ice again and speaks the first words
that will bridge the gap between these two worlds.

"Okay mister, we are not sure what you are all about,
but we are believers in God, and like to think of
ourselves as good Christians, so why don't you have a
seat here, and let's talk about this. Becky, it's going
to be fine. Joey its okay, sit down and be calm."

Aganon slowly walks over and sits at their table, as
he sits down he puts Eddies bible back where Eddie
had it. Slowly, they all sit down, keeping their
distance from Aganon as they do. Nobody takes their
eyes off of him.

Aganon finally speaks as they stare at him in wide
eyed wonder, "Ya'll are my charge, my assignment,
my mission; if you want to call it that. I am not here

to frighten you, or harm you in any way. I am a servant of the Lord of Lords, similar to you. My duties are just different that yours. You all have prayed for clarity in the Word for years, and your prayers have been answered; There is so much power in your prayer, and when you all pray in agreement as a body, the power that you produce is enough to strengthen nations. You must believe me."

 "This is a leap of faith, no doubt about that," Eddie says.

"Tell us something that you could not possibly know, mister," Robbie demands.

"My name is Aganon my young friends," Aganon replies.

"Okay, Aggie, come on tell us something?" Robbie challenges.

"You want proof?" Aganon says.

"Proof would be good," Joseph says.

"The Lord does not permit me to display acts that contradict faith," Aganon replies. "If you will allow me to tell our story, I'm sure all your questions will be answered."

"Okay," Eddie agrees, "We're listening." He looks around at his friends. They all nod in agreement.

"First of all let me set your minds at ease," Aganon begins. "Joseph, you are correct in your observation about my coffee. I was mock consuming the drink, which is very exhilarating, I must add. The coffee was consumed, but displaced in my mouth. I am unable to eat or drink, I do not have the necessary functions to digest like you do. I am an angelic being. Therefore, I do not require food or drink to sustain life. I operate on the power of God through the prayers of His people."

Eddie stares in awe.

"Secondly, I have come in answer to your prayers. All of you have prayed at great length for clarity and enlightenment in regards to the Word of God, and as I told you, the six of you have such faithful prayer coverage that the answered prayer is a great act of faith. Now the six of you have the task to follow through in faith."

Aganon continues. "All of you had one area of the Bible in common for which you sought spiritual growth, the Old Testament.

Aganon takes a moment to let them gather their thoughts and digest what he has shared so far. They look around at each other for a moment, and then turn back to Aganon.

Aganon continues, "If I am to call the six of you my charge, I'll have to know your names."

They sit around the large oval table looking from one to another, then back to Aganon. Finally, Becky stands up.

"Howdy Aganon, I love your coat. My name is Rebecca Stock; everyone calls me Becky, Nice to meet you." Becky holds her hand out to Aganon. Aganon stands up and smiles at Becky. He reaches out and grasps Becky's hand gently but they do not shake hands. They stand there, hands clasped, regarding each other. A moment passes, and then Becky drops her hand and sits down.

She looks at her hand, and says, "My fear is gone, I can see him now."

"You can see who?" Joey says.

"Aggie," Becky says, nodding toward Aganon.

"What do you mean, Becky?" Robbie asks.

"Never mind," Angela says, standing up. She holds her hand out to Aganon. He takes her hand, not shaking hands, just clasped.

"My name is Angela Woods," she says, the fear leaving her voice. "I remember where I have seen you before; you were in the crowd on the beach when I almost drowned in Pituit Lake the summer of my 7th grade year. It was when I saw your face that I woke up. I was unconscious. It was you, wasn't it?"

Aganon just flashes his heart warming smile. Angela sits down with an amazed look on her face.

"What is going on here?" Eddie asks to nobody.

Joey stands up and thrusts his hand out to Aganon, "My name is Joseph Stile, I don't understand what's going on here, but I'm willing to find out." Aganon takes Joeys hand, they slowly shake hands, and then Joey drops his hand and sits down, breathing a large sigh of relief.

Robbie stands up, waits a few moments, and then slowly raises his hand toward Aganon who takes his hand, "My name is Robert Edgar, and I have to admit that I'm not sure I believe you are who you say. I am willing to walk by faith, in Jesus' name. Oh, and everyone calls me Robbie." Robbie drops his hand, looks at it once, and then sits down. He chuckles, and then looks at Laura.

Laura glowers at Robbie then stands up. She looks directly into Aganon's face. She feels warmth fill her as though she has just taken a large sip of hot cocoa. She raises her hand to Aganon. He takes her hand in his.

Advocate of Time   Craig Allan

"My name is Laura Sweet," she says, a grin forming on her face. "I'm not exactly sure what it is you're here to show us. So... as long as it's in line with God's Word, and is not illegal, I guess I'm in.

Laura drops her hand and sits down with a smile brushing her mouth. She looks at Eddie and nods toward Aganon. Eddie nods then stands up, still looking at Laura. He turns to look at Aganon, and stares directly into his eyes. They are the most calming, soft brown eyes he has ever seen in his life. They are solid love. Eddies heart begins to beat faster. He raises his hand to Aganon.

"Hello Aganon, angel of The Most High. My name is Edward Rowl. My friends call me Eddie. I'm a follower of Jesus. I'm very skeptical of false prophets and religions. I am especially leery of cons. I am praying that God will grant me the sight to see you for who you are."

Aganon takes Eddie's hand in his. They stand there, hands clasped, outstretched, and the moments pass. Eddie continues to stare into Aganon's eyes. Then a memory from Eddie's childhood flashes into his mind.

He is seven years old and he's standing on the railroad tracks behind his house. He is looking at the rocks piled up around the ties. There comes a train horn from behind him, he looks to see a train coming. Eddie turns to run off the tracks and his shoe lace gets caught on a railroad spike, Eddie trips and falls onto the tracks. He reaches down to get his shoelace off the spike, and the train comes closer, its horn blaring. Every time he tries to unhook his lace from the spike, it gets looped around it farther. Eddie begins to pull on his foot. He can't get it loose. He looks at the train, now dragging its brakes and sliding toward him, it's only seconds away. He covers his eyes with his arms and drops his head. Suddenly, Eddie feels like he is floating. He opens his eyes, and he sees bright light all around him. He looks up, and sees himself flying toward his bike lying in the grass by the road. He looks back in time to see the train sliding by him, brakes dragging, and grinding. Just before he lands on the grass, he sees a very kind looking man with soft brown eyes carrying him through the air. Landing in the grass, he rolls to a stop two feet from his bike. He sits up, and looks all around him. The man is gone.

The memory fades....

"It was you!" Eddie cries. "You were the one who pulled me from the tracks."

Chapter 3

Demonstration

Aganon holds Eddies gaze.

"Yes Eddie," Aganon replies, "Even then, you were destined for this day. The Almighty would not have you lost."

Eddie begins to weep. Not for the memory of his childhood, but for the hardness of his heart.

Eddie finally sees Aganon for who he is. He drops his hand, sits down, sets his arms on the table, and lowers his head. Nobody speaks for a very long time. Then Aganon speaks.

"You are the central figure in this story, Eddie," Aganon explains. "It was you God chose to work through, to lead you're friends to the cross; then to this very moment and then into spiritual enlightenment. As you know, you have a strong desire to know the historical events of the Bible on a larger scale. What you do not know; and I'd venture to say is the same for all of you, is that while you were praying for greater understanding of God's

Word, He was arranging my visit." Aganon continues, "Which brings me to the reason I am here." Aganon takes Eddies bible and opens it to the book of Exodus. He points at chapter two which describes Moses' birth.

"I have come to guide you into the land of Egypt." Aganon pauses to look at everyone.

Eddie sits up and looks at what Aganon is doing, and for a moment he is confused. Then suddenly, it dawns on him. Eddies mouth drops open.

"Are you saying what I think you are?" he asks.

Aganon looks at Eddie in silence.

"Answer me, Aganon," Eddie demands.

"Eddie, I am an advocate of time," Aganon replies.

"You mean to take us time traveling," Eddie suggests.

Aganon holds his hand up to them, gesturing for them to pause.

"Let me explain how moving in time works," He stands up. "But not here, let's go to the park across the street. I need to get outside, the indoors stifles me."

They look at each other, shrug and pick up their things. Eddie holds his hand up to them and says,

"Hold up, let's pray. We need God's wisdom in this." They bow their heads.

"Lord God. Guide us, and protect us as we seek your will and your wisdom. Help us to see Aganon for who he is, and help us to have faith in your plan, and your will. In Jesus name, Amen"

"Ok, let's go." Eddie puts two dollars on the table and leads the way out.

 They each leave a couple bucks on the table and then one at a time, they move to the door and exit the Webster Study Inn.

Aganon follows his charge out of the diner and across the street into the city park. There are kid's jungle gym toys in a pea gravel pit. Surrounding that is a cement sidewalk. Along the sidewalk are park benches and a few picnic tables scatter about.

Eddie stops at the picnic table closest to the street, keeping a view of the diner just in case they have a problem, but his gut tells him that he is safer than he has ever been in his life. He sets his Bible down on the table, turns toward Aganon, and plops down on the bench.

"Okay Aggie," Eddie says, smiling a bit, "Let's hear how time works."

"Yeah," the others echo.

"Let's hear it," Angel says.

Aganon steps forward as they all sit down. They watch him intently.

He reaches his hand way out in front of him and points his finger, then bends it at the tip just a bit.

"Imagine that time leaves a mark as it passes just like a seismograph does when the earth shakes during an earthquake."

Joey looks at Eddie with a question forming on his lips. "It's the instrument they use to measure earthquakes and has a needle that marks on paper." Eddie makes a fast waving motion with his finger pointed.

"Ahh," Joey says, "Got it."

Aganon looks at them and starts waving his arm up and down, faster and faster, like a seismograph. His hooked finger leaving tracers just like the instrument does. High and low peaks and valleys form in the air in a faint greenish glowing set of lines. His arm goes faster, and faster, then even faster, leaving lines up and down, longer and longer. Then he suddenly stops.

"Now, you see these peaks at the top of these spikes?" He points to the tips of the lines he has drawn in the air.

"These are the high points in time. Major events that are measured in greatness by the people that witness, and record them. Let's say this one is the end of your revolutionary war here in the United States." He points at one spike. "This one is the end of the Civil War. This one, the day World War II ended." He points at the high points on down the line.

"The low points are the negative events in time measured by those who record them. Those are events such as the start of a war, the death of a world leader, disastrous events, and so on." He points at the low peaks on down the line.

"What I do, is skip along the tips of these high, and low events. I do this by creating doorways with these." He opens his coat and holds it out on the sides for them to see his whip, and lariat.

"The portals in time can only be created by using God's creation to mold an opening. No man-made structure or article can be used to open or create a portal." Aganon pauses for a moment to allow this to sink in. "Not only do these portals open on a place in time, but also on a place on earth. For example, we are in the town of Webster, New Mexico. If you were going to travel to Egypt in the time of Moses you would have to travel back in time, as well as to the location where Moses lived, Egypt. All of this is done by the glory and power of the Almighty God. None of this is possible without his divine grace and power. I know this is a lot to grasp all at once, but it's easier if I simply let you all in on what is going on, and right up front. Any questions so far?

Robbie speaks up, "Yeah, I don't know about these guys, but I'm still not convinced Aggie. I don't mean any disrespect, but I'm a skeptic at heart. I allow all of my faith in Jesus, which leaves little else for others. How can we be sure you are not an imposter?"

"By imposter you mean a spirit of darkness, a demon."

"Well, yeah, I guess."

"I have to tell you again, that I am not permitted to offer testimony of myself, only He whom sent me. However, it is within my charge to demonstrate why I have come. Would that be enough to cast your doubts away?"

They nod in agreement.

"Very well, however, this will take an act of faith on someone's part, does not matter who." He gestures to them with his outstretched hand.

Eddie stands up slowly. "What is it you need me to do?"

"Eddie?" Angela whimpers. Eddie holds his hand out to her, and she grasps it briefly, then he steps forward.

"It's quite simple, Eddie. I need you to believe in He who sent me, and believe in my charge."

"What exactly is 'your charge'?" Eddie asks.

"You are my charge Eddie; all of you are my charge. My charge means my mission, my assignment, and those chosen to participate.

"So you need me to believe in God, which is easy; and believe in you," Eddie probes.

"Not me, Eddie, but in yourself, your friends, and the wisdom you seek. All that in mind, you need to believe in the method God himself has chosen."

"Ok. What do I do?"

"First of all, help me locate an object that is born of God, not man."

Advocate of Time   Craig Allan

Eddie looks around the park. At the far north end, past the ball field, is a large cottonwood standing alone; the last surviving tree in that area of the park. The tree is considered by some to be a landmark, and older than the town itself. It was left where it stands for that reason.

Eddie points, "There, that tree has been there forever, and is not influenced, or made by men."

"Very well, shall we go have a look? Come." Aganon gestures to his charge.

They get up and start toward the lone cottonwood, each praying their own silent prayers.

They arrive at the tree and Aganon motions for Eddie to come stand with him.

Eddie stands next to Aganon, facing the tree.

"Ok, now what?"

"Now we travel. Eddie, clear your mind of any doubt and fear. Gather your faith, and let no other thought enter your mind but one. I need you to think of the one place you feel closest to God. It can be any place, at any time." Aganon holds his hand out to Eddie.

"That's an easy one. Camp Pituit, at Lake Pituit, there is a tree at the far end of the lake where we all go sometimes to pray, study, and strengthen our walk with the Lord. We all share the same place." Eddie says, looking at his friends. They nod in unison.

"Good," Aganon nods, still holding his hand out to Eddie, "Now I need the image to do the recall, you must offer it to me. Take my hand please. Remember, Eddie, no doubt, no fear, total faith." Aganon says.

Eddie looks at Aganon's hand, then into his eyes. He sees only hope and love there. Eddie reaches out and takes hold of Aganon's hand. It is so soft; he has to look to make sure it is even there. He closes his eyes and looks in his mind to the tree cove at the end of Lake Pituit. The image comes to mind as clear as if he was there, then it vanishes for a brief moment as if it is erased, then quickly returns. He opens his eyes, and Aganon is looking at him. He is smiling.

"That's a nice place Eddie. God's presence is there."

He opens his coat and draws out his whip. He tosses is out in front of him. As it unravels across the ground, Eddie notices that it appears to have a golden shine to it, and woven so tightly, it could almost be made of fine thread. The very end appears to have some sort of icon woven into the material to create the tip. Eddie looks closer and notices that it is a small cross, possibly made of dense wood. The handle appears to be made of the same dense wood;

he thinks it must be sandalwood. The tool is beautiful. No doubt that it has divine influence.

"Now, let me show you why I have come, and how we shall go," Aganon says, looking up at the nearest limb on the old cottonwood tree. He draws it back with blinding speed then whips it upward toward the branch. The whips tail flying through the air creates a whistling sound that none of them have ever heard before. *Later they will all agree that it resembled what could only be described as a high pitch angelic sound, like singing.* As the end of the whip wraps around the middle of the tree limb, Aganon pulls back quickly, drawing tension in the whip and creating a taught line between his outstretched arm and the tree limb.

As they all watch in awe, he gestures toward the enclosed area he has created between the whip, the limb, the tree, and the ground.

"Observe," Aganon says. They watch intently at nothing but thin air. Then, very faintly, they see a bluish swirling pool in the center of the area where Aganon is pointing. The pool begins to swirl faster, and grow larger in size. They can barely see some sort of figure in the swirling blue of the pool. As it grows larger then begin to see the tree they have sat around so many times, for so many years. That tree is the centerpiece of their sacred place; the place where they go to be close God, alone with Him. It's the tree cove at the end of Lake Pituit. Eddie gapes in awe and amazement as the swirl of the pool begins to dissipate and the tree and lake in the background come into clear focus.

Eddie takes a step toward the image, noticing the ripples of the lake, and the light wake of waves washing on the shore. It's not an image.

"The water is moving." Eddie says in awe. "It's not a vision or picture, it's the real thing."

"You bet it is, Eddie," Aganon replies. "Just like the image you showed me."

Laura stands up and points. "Eddie, there's our sign, right there on the tree. It's still there." The sign on the tree reads: 'God's place'

"Yep, that's it alright, I'm so glad it's still there," Robbie says. "When was it you made that sign, Joey, Seventh grade?"

"Eighth." Joey answers; still in awe.

"Is this real, Eddie?" Becky asks.

"I think so. I think Aganon is exactly what he says he is." Eddie says.

"Shall we step in?" Aganon suggests.

They stand where they are, staring at Aganon.

"Remember, this is an act of faith. I did not open this portal to prove anything to you, except to show you the function of my tools. This is the unveiling; the steps to travel must be yours. You must call upon your faith in God Almighty and yourselves." Aganon pauses then says, "Ready when you are."

Eddie steps toward the portal, and Laura calls gently to him.

"Eddie?" she questions.

"It's okay Laura. I'll be fine, just watch closely and be ready, keep your faith in God and most important, don't stop praying." Eddie flashes his warmest smile and winks, with that he turns and steps through the portal. The image ripples away from where he steps through as though it were water. Eddie can be seen on the other side, next to the tree. He is touching the sign that Joey made in eighth grade.

Angela walks around behind the portal to look at it. It isn't there; no lake, no Eddie, no tree; only her friends, the grass, the end of the park, and in the distance the city of Webster. She steps back in front of the portal, looks at the others, turns toward the image of Eddie at the lake, and steps through the portal. As she comes through on the other side, she stumbles and Eddie catches her. She looks back at

44

the others and nods. They look once more at
Aganon; he nods and flashes his winning smile. One
at a time they walk through. Robbie is the last one
through and Aganon follows him, and with a flick of
his wrist, the whip comes down behind him and trails
through the portal. The portal shrinks in size exactly
the way it was born. It decays, and swirls showing a
fading image of Aganon and his charge standing
under a tree at the end of Lake Pituit. Then the image
fades to nothingness and the portal is gone.

Nothing is left in the far end of the park under the
cottonwood tree; only the night and the silence.

Chapter 4

Lake Pituit

"Are we standing in Eddie's memory of this place?" Angela asks.

"No Angela. We are at Lake Pituit, at the very moment you all walked through the portal." Aganon replies.

"So, it's Friday April 6th," She glances at her watch, "7:55pm right here, right now?"

"Yes it is, in fact, if you'll notice your watch again, you may understand better."

She looks at her watch again, watching it intently. Then her mouth gapes open, and she taps her watch several times, and then puts it to her ear.

"I can hear it ticking, but it's stopped moving. Why did it stop, but still ticks?" She asks, confused.

"Because time has stopped for us," Eddie interjects. "Once we stepped through that portal, we were stepping into this location at that very moment in

46

time. My guess is time has stopped for us, but not for this place."

"Very good Eddie, you are catching on. Time passes here, but not for all of you. You do not age, and time does not pass. When we re-open Eddies portal to the park, it will be as if we walked right through, and only the time passed that it took to take the steps through."

"That's too wild," Robbie says in amazement.

"Totally," Joey agrees.

"There are many levels of this sort of travel my friends. Let me try to explain a little of how it works. This particular place is a memory of Eddie's. However, it is not an ongoing event, or time peak like I explained in the park. It was generated by way of a memory, so it is stagnant. It does not flow like the events of time do. Even though the water is moving, and the night is alive. This place in time is motionless." Aganon explains.

"Uh, so what exactly does that mean Aggie?" Joey asks.

"It means that we are in a loop in time that is not moving. We are here at this part of the lake at 7:55pm just like we were fifteen minutes ago when we got here. So if somebody walks by this spot of the lake at 7:56pm they will not see us." Eddie explains. "Is that about right Ag?"

"Pretty much; that's the simple version. The specific version is that it is 7:55 pm and twelve seconds, one hundred twenty five hundredths, and so on, and so on down to the split second. We came through at an exact millisecond in time. So if someone would have been standing right here, our passing in to this moment of time would have passed so quickly, they would not have seen us at all."

"Ok, now I know I'm tripping out." Robbie says, in exasperation.

"This is totally cool." Joey says.

"Yes, but a little scary to," Laura whispers, "This is not normal."

Aganon touches her shoulder, comforting her. "It's true that this is not a normal activity Laura, but I assure you, this is inspired by God, and it is His power that makes it possible, as I draw my power from your prayers to God. So in essence, it is you, all of you, which make this possible. You are perfectly safe."

"So let me get this straight," Becky says, stepping up to Aganon, "We could stay right here for a month if we wanted to, and if we went back through that portal we would come through it on the other side as though we passed right through, and no time would have passed there, even though a month passed here."

"You got it Becky." Aganon says.

"Wow," Becky sighs, "God is amazing."

"Amen," they echo.

"Now let's talk about where ya'll wanna to go." Aganon says.

"Aganon," Angela giggles, "You're really starting to play the part."

"What do ya mean, Angela?"

"What I mean Ag is that you said 'ya'll' twice since we got to the park, but when you first got here, you were talking like a college professor. You're speech patterns are beginning to reflect your outfit. You are starting to sound like a Texas cowpoke," Angela explains, "which is pretty cool."

"Aw shucks missy, that's the nicest thang anyone's ever said t'me." Aganon says in a John Wayne western drawl. Eddie and the others burst out laughing, they laugh for a few minutes; and just like that, the circle of six friends has become seven.

"So we are all in agreement that we'll travel with Ag across time?" Eddie proposes. "We have to be agreed as a group. We are a team. I know I'm in."

"Count me in to," Angela says.

"Me too," says Laura.

"Yep," Robbie says, giving thumbs up.

"Sure, sounds like an adventure," Joey agrees.

Everyone looks at Becky waiting for her response to the vote. Aganon looks off at Camp Pituit. He cannot sway her decision in any way, so he must not look at her until she has made her decision. Becky looks down at the ground, then up at her friends.

"This is totally up to you Becky," Eddie explains, "We are a group, a team. We only go if you agree, there is no pressure; this is as much your choice as it is ours."

She looks at Eddie, then at the others and says,

"I'm all for it guys, it's just that I want to go see Moses in the book of Exodus that we have studying for the last few weeks." Becky says, in a timid tone.

"Of course we can go see Moses, I think that's a great idea Becky," Angela says.

"Yeah, it sure is," Eddie says.

Aganon turns back toward his charge and gestures for them to gather close. They huddle together around the base of the tree in the cove at the end of the lake. They sit down and make a plan to meet back at the park tomorrow night at 8:00pm to make their journey into Old Testament Egypt. When they have finished planning the era and location they stand up and gather in a circle, including Aganon. They bow their heads and say a fervent prayer for their protection, guidance, enlightenment, and courage.

"Ok ya'll, let's get a move on." Aganon says. "Are we ready to go back?"

"Let's do it Aggie." Joey says, winking to Aganon.

Aganon draws his whip, pulls it back and sends it sailing up and around a high limb above their heads.

"For our return, in Jesus blessed name," He prays. Then he nods toward the doorway he has created. The portal begins to swirl in the center, and slowly grows toward the outer edges of his doorway. They can begin to see the old cottonwood in the back field of the park. The portal finally swirls to a placid pool with the scene of the park in perfect view.

"You first Eddie, then Angela, everyone back through the way you came in, Robbie last." Aganon explains. "Onward Christian soldiers!"

They all grin, and one at a time, they walk back through the portal, after Robbie is through Aganon steps in, flicks his wrist to retrieve his whip, and steps through. The portal fades and winks out of existence.

On the other side Eddie steps through the grass under the cottonwood, then Angela, one at a time they walk in single file until Aganon walks through the grass behind Robbie. They stop and all turn back to look at Aganon, who is standing exactly where the first portal was. He is rolling up his whip and hangs it back on his belt. He closes his coat.

"Now we all understand what it is that I am here to do?" He asks.

"Yes Ag, we finally understand, and we have faith." Angela says. Everyone nods in agreement.

Then we are well met. I shall leave you to the remainder of your evening, and will meet you here tomorrow night at exactly this time. Angela looks at her watch; it is exactly 8:00 pm.

"Wow, it's exactly 8:00 o'clock only 5 minutes have passed." She says, in amazement. They all look at her watch, each uttering their amazement. When Angela looks up to tell Aganon they'll meet up tomorrow night, he is gone.

"Wow, he's gone." She says. Eddie looks up. Aganon is nowhere to be found.

"He sure gets around." Eddie says. "So what do you guys think? Are we up for this?"

"I'm game." Angela says. They all nod in agreement.

"Okay, let's say a quick prayer, and then we'll head back to the diner and get ourselves home." Eddie suggests. They gather in a circle and grasp each other hands, and in agreement as one body, they pray for God's wisdom in their mission, they pray for His guidance, and His protection. They pray for a safe journey, and they pray for Aganon. When they have finished they hug each other, walk back to the diner, get in their cars and head home.

From atop the diner, Aganon watches their prayer, and is empowered and charged by it. He looks out to the expanse of the sky and says,

"Lord Almighty, Lamb of God, Alpha and Omega; May I keep my charge well, and let your name be praised." He speaks to his maker, "Thank you for the opportunity to work with these faithful of your children."

Chapter 5

Ancient Egypt

8:00 pm sharp Aganon sits on the limb of the cottonwood. He watches as his charge arrive at the diner one at a time. They cross to the park and stand around the picnic table where they sat last night watching Aganon explain the high and low points in time. They pray. Then, as a solid group, they cross the back field of the park toward the old cottonwood where Aganon waits.

As they approach the tree, Aganon jumps down and waits for them under the tree. They smile as they come up to him. Glad to see him again. Aganon is happy to see them as well.

"Howdy Ag, good to see ya pardner." Joey says, with a western drawl.

"Howdy Joey," He replies in like manner. "Howdy everyone, glad y'all decided to come along. This will be a marvelous journey."

"We wouldn't miss it for the world Ag," Eddie proclaims.

"Do we need to bring anything Ag?" Angela asks, "We have a few things; a couple bags and some fanny packs too. We were not sure how this goes, so we just kinda winged it."

"Whatever you bring will be fine; all your basic needs will always be met." Aganon replies. "You all need to be clear on a few points of this particular type of travel. Last night, we traveled to a location brought about by a memory. This time, we are going to an actual set of events in time. This will be real time, not a loop in time, but the actual moving of events. We will blend into their time, we will appear to be among them, yet they will not be able to interact with us, unless we first interact. We are sealed in another level of time until we make contact. We must never make contact. I must stress this point. We can in no way disrupt, or disturb any event in the flow of time, this can be catastrophic. We are only observers. We are gathering knowledge and enlightenment, we are not to interfere."

He pauses "Do we all understand this very important point?"

"Of course," Eddie says. They all nod in agreement.

"What would happen if we were to disturb something Ag?" Becky asks.

"It would cause a ripple effect that would pass through time all the way to current events, and would compound at each high and low point in time, it would be disastrous." He emphasizes, "We must never get involved, no matter what. I cannot stress that enough."

"Okay Ag," Becky says.

"That being said; the rest will come as we go. Remember that we stick together, and we do not interact with anything." Ag reiterates. "Now, where do we start, have you agreed on a starting point?"

"Yep," Eddie says, "We want to start at Moses' birth."

"Very well, the second chapter of Exodus, we'll see so much more than the book offers. This will be exciting."

Aganon opens his coat, draws his whip, and draws it back. He glances at his charge, winks at Joey and lets it fly. It lands around the same limb, and wraps up. He pulls it tight, and creates the doorway. The portal blinks into existence. Suddenly there is a scene of a city of old, with houses made of sod brick, mortar, and sand. Streets made of rock, and brick. They see people wandering through the streets, and far at the end of the street is a labor camp where dark skinned people are working under heavy burden.

"Hey Ag," Robbie speaks up, "I have a quick question. What is the rope for?"

Aganon grins at Robbie, "It serves the same function pardner, and it's simply a different tool. I can use it on larger objects, like big rocks, large trees, things like that." Aganon explains.

"Oh, ok. Robbie says.

"Ok, so who's ready to make a trip to Egypt?" Aganon asks.

"I guess it's now or never, huh." Becky says. She walks up to the portal, looks at Aganon, winks, and steps through. The portal drops out between two buildings in a very narrow alley. Becky has to turn slightly to go farther into the alleyway and allow for the others to come through. Eddie goes next, then Angela, then Laura, Robbie next, and last is Joey. Aganon gently squeezes Joey's shoulder as he steps up to the portal. It reassures him and he steps through. Aganon looks around the park then back to the portal. He steps through and flicks his whip back and down. The portal winks closed behind him. The air stirs faintly where the portal has winked out, and then there is calm and quiet.

In one short step they are in the land of Egypt at the time of Moses birth. Their clothing has been transformed to the clothing of the time. Even their skin tone has darkened enough so they can blend in. Angela is the first to notice.

"Look at our clothes, and our skin," She giggles.

"Your attire will always be changed to that of the time and place," Aganon says, "even your appearance and skin tone will blend in. All part of God's plan.

Aganon beckons for them to gather close, they gather around.

"Now remember, nobody here can see you, but if you make contact, then you will break through our level of time, directly into theirs. So stay close." Aganon explains. "Follow me." He sets out down the street toward the labor camp where the slaves are working.

As they approach the end of the street Laura speaks in a hushed tone,

"Ag, are you sure they can't see us?"

"Yes Laura, I'm sure. If we pass by their peripheral vision, they might be able to notice a faint shadow, or movement, but when they look directly at us, they will see nothing. We exist approximately ten milliseconds in time before them. So technically, we are not really here yet. Just enough to see what is happening." Aganon replies.

"Ugh, time can be totally confusing." She says in exasperation.

They stop at the end of the street watching the slaves working in the brick foundry and labor yard.

"So the Egyptians made the children of Israel serve with rigor. And they made their lives bitter with hard bondage-in mortar, in brick, and in all manner of service in the field. All their service in which they made them serves was with rigor." Eddie quoted.

"Exodus chapter one, verses thirteen and fourteen." Angela confirmed. "We were just studying those passages last night. This is so amazing."

"It's so sad; the Pharaoh dealt such pain and suffering on these people, and for nothing but his own fear of the one true God." Laura says. They nod in agreement.

They watch soberly as the slaves work and toil under the punishment of the taskmasters. Finally, they cannot watch any longer and they turn away, one by one. Aganon comforts them saying, "Now you know a bit of how our God has felt. Yet His people endured, and became stronger, and they multiplied. It is written."

They stand in their tight little group; safe, secure, and silent. Finally one of them breaks the silence.

"Where is Moses, Ag?" Becky asks.

"He is born this hour to the house of Levi." He replies. "Let's go see him."

Aganon steps back and beckons. He leads as they make their way along the slave quarters, looking for the house where Moses will be born. They come to the end of the narrow passage and stop in front of a small building that appears to house many people. Aganon stops short at the doorway, and they almost run him over. He turns to them and says, "Remember, touch nothing, touch no one." He enters through the doorway that has only a curtain for a door. They follow him in, and they stop in a small front room that has two stairways going upward and two doorways with curtains for doors. They take a moment to allow their eyes to adjust to the dark.

Aganon points at the stairway on the left side of the room. Then he starts up, and they follow. In a dimly lit room with folded piles of linen on the floor for beds, they find a woman holding a newborn baby. Standing over her is a thin, but muscular man. He is looking at them lovingly, but with great dread on his face. He whispers something to the woman. Her expression of joy turns to pain and sorrow. The woman begins to weep in deep and sorrowful sobs. She holds the baby close to her, kissing its head, and crying. The man touches her shoulder, kneels down beside her, and holds her and the baby. They sit like that for what seems like an eternity. Finally Angela turns away and speaks in a whisper to Aganon.

"Why do they look so sad Ag? Do they fear for his life? He is in danger, isn't he?"

"Yes Angela," Aganon answers in a reverent tone. "The midwife that was ordered by Pharaoh to kill this Hebrew child failed to follow through. But she did not fail to warn them that Egyptian soldiers would be searching the city regularly for their surviving sons. Their child is not safe, and they know it."

"Yes," Eddie agrees. "The Pharaoh was worried that the numbers of Hebrews would outnumber the Egyptians soon, and they would generate an army against him. So he ordered all the sons of the Hebrews drowned in the Nile. The midwives disobeyed Pharaohs orders because they fear God more than Pharaoh. Pharaoh is aware of this as well. He will send his soldiers."

"She will hide him for about three months until she can no longer, then she will do the only thing she knows to do." Laura continues. "She will build a tiny ark and float him down the river in hopes someone will find him, and she will set his sister to watch."

"The scriptures tell us that Pharaohs daughter will find him, she will see Miriam, Moses sister, standing close by and will order her to find a Hebrew woman to nurse the child, and his sister will go get his mother for the task. Then the princess will pay his mother to raise this baby as her own until he is through the weaning years. That is when she will take him as her own, adopt him, and he will be called Moses, meaning drawn out of the water."

"You all have studied well." Aganon commends them. "That is correct, he will be called Moses, and he will be raised in the courts of Pharaoh. His true mother will instruct him about who he really is and that he is of the Hebrew people, but he must stay alive by growing of age in the courts of the royals," Aganon continues. "Someday, he will come to a difficult decision." Aganon turns away from Moses and his parents, and then gathers his charge around him. "Let's move on to the river banks where the princess finds Moses."

They follow Aganon out of the house and up the street to a hillside, scattered with rocks and boulders. Aganon draws his lariat this time. He swings it in the air over his head, every time it passes over his head; the loop grows larger until finally it is large enough for him to release it. With a lightning fast pump of his arm he lets fly with the lariat and it sails through the air, producing a high pitched hum that sounds like pure harmony. The loop lands over a rock outcropping not more than eight feet away from him, and with a flick of his wrist he draws the rope tight, creating a doorway between him, the rock, the rope, and the ground. He glances at the doorway, and the image begins to wink into existence and then appears instantly. The scene is over the river that borders the slave quarters they are overlooking. It's the Nile, three months from now. In the image, they can see a small object caught in the reeds and a woman with others gathered near to her walking near the reeds.

"There he is," Eddie shouts, pointing at the scene and then he lunges into the portal.

"Eddie!" Angela cries, running after him, the others follow them in, and Aganon brings up the rear, drawing his lariat in with a flick of his wrist as he passes through. The portal wavers, and then winks out of existence. The air stirs in a tiny dust devil where they stood seconds before, and then moves down the hillside. Then, nothing else stirs. They are gone.

Eddie walks toward the river bank a mere five feet from where the princess and her maids are looking down at a tiny ark. Aganon holds him back, and they watch in awe. The princess motions for one of her maids to bring the ark up to the shore. The maid does as she is bidden and the princess bends down and removes the covering. They gasp in unison as they find a healthy three month old baby staring back at them from the ark. The princess draws close to the baby, and he begins to cry. She feels drawn to his need and picks him up. She says to her maids that this has to be a Hebrew child. Moses sister, watching from near the reeds approaches the princess and asks if she should go find a nurse from the Hebrew women for her to care for this child. The princess tells her "Go." So Moses' sister brings their mother to be the child's nurse. The princess tells the Hebrew woman to care for the child through his weaning years, and she will pay her a wage.

"Ag, I just noticed that we are able to understand their language perfectly, in fact, they are speaking English with perfect clarity." Joey says, in amazement.

"All part of the transforming to the age my friends." Aganon replies.

"I love the irony in this situation." Angela exclaims. "The Pharaohs daughter; who was party to the royals plan to kill all the newborn sons of Israel, is now going to pay a wage to Moses' mother to care for a child she will call her own, when her father had intended for him to be drowned in the river."

"God is good, and His mercy endures forever." Becky exalts.

"Amen to that sister," Robbie agrees.

"Alright time travelers, where do ya'll want to go now?" Aganon drawls.

Eddie looks at his friends them he motions for them to gather together. They have a short conference among themselves, and come to an agreement. Eddie speaks for them.

"We want to see what actually happens when Moses witnesses the Hebrew man being beaten, and what causes him to kill the Egyptian taskmaster."

"My friends that is a violent event, although not as horrible as some of the events of this age, there is violence there. Moses kills a man." Aganon instructs. "Are you certain you want to see that?"

"Yes, we are sure Ag." Eddie confirms. "We have agreed." They all nod.

"Very well," He says, walking toward an olive tree growing near the river. He looks back at the women standing near the reeds going on about the baby Moses. He then looks up at a fork in the tree toward the top, draws his whip. He looks back at his charge one more time to be sure they wish to go where he will take them. They nod for him to proceed. Aganon nods back. He draws back his whips and lets it sail to the fork in the tree. As the whips end wraps around the tree just below the fork, he draws it back in a flick of his wrist and the whip pulls tight. This time, he has created a triangular doorway, still allowing plenty of room for the portal to form. He looks into the center of the doorway, and an image begins to slowly come into focus near the center, suddenly blinking into existence.

They see a man standing over another man with his hand raised over his head. His hand is holding a flail with several tails at its end. He is whipping the man. Eddie and the others look on somberly for a moment, then one at a time, they pass through the portal, Aganon sighs, and follows them. He pulls his whip back to him with a flick of his wrist. The whip trails into the portal behind him. The portal wavers, and winks out of existence, leaving nothing in its place. Not even a wisp of wind.

Chapter 6

Moses' life in Egypt

Eddie and Angela hold each other tightly. Robbie, Laura, Becky, and Joey stand behind Aganon. They are peeking around his broad frame, watching as the man in the sand is being beaten by the taskmaster. He is being beaten to death. They can see in the Egyptians facial expression that he fully intends to kill this man. He will not stop. The Hebrew man in the sand is barely flinching anymore with the blows by the tailed flail. The Egyptian is sweating heavily, and blood is mixing with the sweat on his arms, dripping into the sand.

Aganon and his charge are frozen in horror.

Laura asks through her sobs, "Ag, can't you do anything? Can't any of us do something?" Her tone mentions that she already knows they cannot.

"No Laura!" Aganon responds sternly, "we can never intervene with anything here. It would change the events of history so drastically; none of us may even survive its outcome. There is nothing we can do but watch."

As they watch in horror a man rushes by so closely, he nearly runs right through them. He grasps the taskmasters arm in mid swing and spins him around so violently that he stumbles and falls. The man is Moses, and he is enraged with fury. As he stands over the taskmaster, several women rush up and carry the beaten man away. He is barely alive. The taskmaster is winded, and weakened from his rigorous flailing of the Hebrew man. However, his anger has fueled in him a new strength, and he gets to his feet. The taskmaster faces Moses. He draws his knife, pointing it at Moses.

"You," he shouts. "Moses! You shall pay dearly for interfering with the King's taskmaster!"

Moses looks around him and sees no one; even the beaten man is gone. They are alone.

"Use your weapons against me then, taskmaster of the King!" Moses challenges.

The taskmaster draws his knife back and lunges at Moses in an attempt to cut him across the neck. Moses dodges this attack easily. He has been trained in combat arts in the Kings courts, and this man is no match for him. As the taskmaster misses his attack, Moses grasps his outstretched arm by the wrist. He whirls under the taskmasters arm so that his right shoulder is under the taskmaster's outstretched arm.

He pulls down hard on the taskmasters arm and he loses his grip on the knife. Moses takes the knife, and before he has a chance to consider his next move, he whirls again and thrusts it into the side of the taskmaster's neck, killing him instantly. The man crumples in the sand, dead. Moses stands over his body for a moment, and then looks around, suddenly realizing what he has done. He drags the man to the far end of the courtyard where the wall is short. There he rolls him up and over the wall, pulls him to an area where the sand is soft and deep, and buries him. Moses looks around one more time, and then flees.

Aganon and his charge stand where they are for a long time. Finally Aganon steps forward and faces his charge.

"I have nothing to offer on this event, it happened as it did. Moses did not kill out of desire, but in defense of his people. It is written."

"Let's be gone from this place." Aganon commands. He turns and leads them up the nearby stairs that lead to the main corridor. They walk past the slave quarters and up the street where they first saw Moses. Nobody speaks or even looks around. They all stare downward, each keeping their own silent thoughts and prayers. They have only themselves to thank for what they just witnessed. Yet, they all somehow felt drawn to that event, as though they were intended to witness it. Aganon leads them to the hillside where they had created a portal from a rock outcropping. There he sits down.

"This is a good place to gather your thoughts, and take some time to let The Lord speak to you. It will be your decision where we go from here." He says. Becky and Robbie watch Aganon as he sits down to gather his thoughts for their next move. Eddie, Angela, Laura, and Joey gather around the rock outcropping and join hands. They bow their heads in silent prayer. When they finish, they gather around Aganon, each of them sitting silently, taking the time to reflect. Aganon takes in the surroundings. They are on the southeastern hillside of the city. The river runs to the northeast on the other side of town. The Mediterranean Sea is to the north. The day is getting late, and the sun is setting. It has been hot the last few summers but the temperature today is mild. Aganon gets to his feet, turns toward town, takes a few steps down the hill then turns back to his charge.

Aganon tells them, "We will need some food, and then we'll rest for the night in that empty house over there. You would all do very well to stay here and wait for me to return. I will not be long." He sets out toward the market a few hundred yards to the north. He takes the time to reflect on what they have witnessed so far, and what more is to come in the story of Moses. Aganon wonders to himself if they will even want to go on with their journey. He continues down the street, allowing Gods will to guide him.

Eddie looks out over the city and prays silently to himself. "Lord God, if this is your will for us, why do I feel so awful about what we saw?" He asks. A thought returns to him, offering him some comfort and understanding, it is Gods answer to his question. "God has given us free will: the desire to change the course of our lives, and seek wisdom to enlighten our minds. This is the very enlightenment I prayed for." The thought ends with a quote from the book of Mathew chapter seven, verse seven: "Ask and it will be given to you; seek, and you will find; knock and it will be opened to you." Eddie thinks that those were the very words Jesus spoke, and they could not be truer in this case. These answers to his prayer set his mind at ease. He prays "Lord God, grant to us the strength to endure the things we have seen, and the courage to continue in our quest for wisdom, in Jesus precious name, amen."

"Amen brother," Angela says in agreement.

Joey looks over at Eddie, then gets up and walks to where he is sitting. Becky and Joey get up and follow him. Angela and Laura notice them coming and turn to meet them.

They all huddle together around the rock outcropping and wait silently for one of them to speak. Angela breaks the silence.

"Well, I guess it's time we have ourselves a powwow."

"I have prayed about what we have seen so far, and I still have peace about where we are, and what we have planned." Eddie offers in confidence.

"This is no small thing guys," Robbie offers, "We just saw Moses, the prophet of the ten commandments murder another man. We have to be aware that he not only killed the man, but actually took the time to look and make sure nobody was watching when he did. He may not have plotted to do it, but he certainly intended to when he confronted him."

"Yes Robbie," Joey replies, "We are all aware of that, we saw it to. However, this is no surprise to us. It is written just as it happened. We have always known that Moses intentionally killed that taskmaster."

"Yeah," Robbie responds sharply, "But it doesn't make it any easier to stomach. Knowing about it, reading about it, and actually witnessing it, are completely different things."

"Are you regretting coming Robbie?" Eddie asks. "We did vote, and agree to this quest man."

"No Eddie," Robbie replies, "I have no regret, I'm just venting about it, it helps me to talk about things. I'm still praying for understanding as well."

Laura touches Robbie's shoulder, comforting him. He responds with his hand on hers. He looks at her, smiling.

"I think we can all agree that this has been a pretty difficult first day. However, we must remember that it is just the beginning. Are we all still in agreement about what we are doing here, and what is to come?"

They look at each other, and without hesitation, they nod in agreement. They know this is what they have come here for. They have no regrets. They bow their heads, and Eddie leads them in a prayer of strength, wisdom, forgiveness, and thanksgiving. When they have finished their prayer to God, they turn toward the city and await Aganon's return. As the sun sets in the west, they see Aganon coming up the street with a pack in each hand. He comes up the hill, walks into their small circle and hands one pack to Laura, and the other to Becky.

Aganon sits down in the circle and looks to the sky. He says, "Thanks be to the Lord of Hosts. Worthy is the Lamb who was slain." His charge echoes his supplication.

"Worthy is the Lamb," They say in unison.

"Have we all come to understand the events of this day, and given the uncertainty over to God?" He asks of them.

"We have, and we are prepared to continue on our quest for enlightenment and wisdom." Eddie answers for them all.

"Very good, now, let's get something to eat. Tomorrow, we will watch Moses flee the city. Then we'll travel to the days when he was raising his family in Madian, and shepherding. We'll see him speak with the Almighty God in the burning bush, and we'll watch his return to Raamses to set God's people free.

They eat of the packs: Fresh fruit, loaves of bread, and bags of water drawn from fresh wells. They talk of their day, the days to come, and what they hope to learn of God's plan for them. Before they bed down in the empty building on the outer hillside of town, they speak of their charge. Aganon explains of his wanderings in his past; those things he is permitted to speak of, and how he has come to respect the members of the human race that worship and lift up the Lord on High. They forget of the horrible act they witnessed that day, and find kinship among Aganon's presence. They begin to understand, and accept, his charge, and their own as well. They finish up their long evening together, and wander down to the building they will sleep in. They find it to be fairly polluted; riddled with all sorts of rotting foods, and broken down furnishings. They decide that sleeping on the hillside under the stars would be much more appealing. They fall asleep under the stars, feeling closer to God, and more accepting of Aganon; God's chosen advocate to bring them closer to His vast, and unending story.

Chapter 7

Moses' return

Eddie wakes with dew on his clothing and his face. He is rejuvenated in a way he has never felt before. He sits up and finds Aganon already up. He is squatting a few yards up the hill in front of a tiny fire and watching the sun rise on the eastern bank of the hills surrounding the city. His face is lit with the soft orange glow of the new day, and he appears to be singing. Aganon tosses tiny sticks of wood into his little fire, and sings praises to the Lord while he watches the new day dawn. He sees movement on his left. Eddie is approaching; he looks like a brilliant reflection of the human race in the light of the new day and Aganon tells him so.

"Good day Edward, you look brilliant in the suns glow. The new day looks good on you."

"Brilliant huh, "Eddie chuckles, "I don't know if I would say I feel brilliant, but I sure do feel good; like I have been recharged."

"You have been." Aganon confirms.

"How so Aganon, err, Ag?"

"This world has more of what is good, and less of what is not. Think about it." Aganon challenges. "Imagine what life would be like several thousand years in the past, before industry, pollution, and the fall of man."

"Yeah, I never even thought about it. It's like the freshest air possible. It's the way the world used to be, before man learned how to destroy it." Eddie reflects. "Wow, so much we can learn while being here." He closes his eyes, breathes in deeply, and lets out a breath of appreciation.

"Indeed Edward, err, Eddie." Aganon agrees.

They laugh quietly together for a moment, then fall silent, enjoying the warmth of the small fire, and the growing sunrise. Slowly, the others wake, and come to sit around the fire, watching the sun come up over the city. They all appear to be recharged in a way they know they have never experienced before.

Angela speaks up first, "It's this place, isn't it Ag." She queries. "It has an abundance of good air, and a lack of pollutants like we have at home."

Aganon just nods. He notices that none of them are yawning, or even act as though they are still tired. They have probably slept better than they have in their whole lives. They will have trouble re-adjusting to their home climate; just one more aspect of their quest.

They rummage through what is left of the food in the packs, eat a meager but fulfilling breakfast of what is probably the best, and most natural food they have ever eaten. After they have finished, they gather their belongings, clean themselves up, and prepare for the events to come. Aganon is crouching near the rock outcropping as his charge prepares for their day. As Becky finishes brushing her teeth, she notices that Aganon has not had a need for any of the hygiene customs that they do.

Becky says sarcastically, "Must be nice Ag."

"What's that Rebecca?" He replies.

"Psshh! Please, it's Becky, nothing else. I'm talking about the fact that you don't have any of the tedious routines to care for your body like us humans do, must be nice." She chuckles.

Aganon considers her comment, and smiles saying, "I suppose not having to deal with the bodily care rituals has its high points Becky; but I can assure you, not being human, having a command and being made a servant is not a thing to be considered appealing. It is, however, my existence and I accept it with gladness. I thank the Almighty that I am not burdened with envy and jealousy as was Lucifer and his angels. He was not only jealous of Christ, but of you as well. Did you know that?"

Becky shakes her head and Aganon continues. "To be human," Aganon pauses, and then continues to speak a bit slowly, "just to have a mortal life and to choose where your life takes you. That is a very desirable trait my friend. Not another creature in existence shares that gift the way humans do. It is quite unique." Aganon explains.

Becky's face falls, "Ag, I'm sorry. I didn't mean to..." She stammers.

"No Becky, do not apologize. I'm not of despair; I am simply explaining the order of the beings. I am neither offended, nor bothered. Please, do not feel badly." He takes her by the shoulders and embraces her.

"You are a beautiful creature Becky. Do you know that?" He asks softly.

"And so are you Aganon," She returns. "You have brought us such a gift, we are thankful to you."

"I am only the messenger Becky, a servant," He says, stepping back to speak to her. "I am doing what my Lord has charged me with, but I do it with joy and I take great pleasure in being part of your journey."

"You are so much more to us than just a messenger servant Ag." She replies. "You have become a good friend, you are one of us."

"Is what you say true?" Aganon asks.

They all nod as they look on to Becky and Aganon's conversation. Aganon looks at them one by one, and smiles like a school boy then they laugh together for a few moments.

Becky pats Aganon on the shoulder and goes back to her belongings to finish packing up.

Aganon just continues smiling.

One at a time; they finish getting their things together, then gather around Aganon and prepare to set out into town to see Moses' next move. They move confidently down the hillside and into the street. Looking nothing like the sight of the night before; bewildered and lost. This is a group of people who know where they are going, and what they must do.

The bright day finds merchants in the market milling around; exchanging stories of the day before where they witnessed the son of the princess kill a taskmaster in defense of a Hebrew man. As the merchants talk among themselves, Moses is walking through the market, looking around, and hearing stories of the event of the day before. He finds two men fighting and asks them why they quarrel amongst themselves when they should be standing together as a tribe. One of the quarrelling men says to Moses, "Who made you the prince, and judge of us? Do you intend to kill me as you killed the Egyptian?" Moses says, "Surely this thing is known." In fear that Pharaoh would seek to kill him, he rushes out of the market. As Moses pushed past the crowds of merchants, he passes a faint shadow on the wall leading up the stairs. He glances toward the corner of the wall in fear there would be a guard or soldier there watching him, but there is nobody there. He hurries up the steps and into the inner city where he must gather what little he can carry, and flee the city. He will seek a hiding place in the lands to the east.

Aganon and his charge watch as Moses flees the market, then brushes past them, stops and looks directly at them. He is a young man, with a short beard and long hair. He looks frightened, and desperate. He wastes no time looking at them. He hurries up the stairs and out of sight. Laura turns to Aganon with a look of astonishment.

"Did you see that Ag? He looked right at us." She says in excitement.

"Yes Laura," He replies, "but it was only a faint shadow he saw, I'm sure he thought we were somebody else. It was us he was seeing, although we were not really there. He is so distracted right now, a man on the run. He will be for many years to come." Aganon continues, "He is in God's hands now."

"It happened just as it is written," Eddie confirms, "right to the very words the Hebrew man says. This is so amazing! Where to now? Ag."

"We have a good area to use for travel, so let's go back to the hillside and set out to meet up again with Moses in the land of Midian." He turns toward the inner city and sets out across town toward their hillside. They follow him closely through the city.

At the rock outcropping, Aganon tosses his lariat outward, and loops the rock easily. He pulls the rope tight, gestures toward the long rectangular doorway, once again. The image in the center begins to wink into existence, wavering slightly, then suddenly; as before, it appears as though it were a scene in a movie. The image is of a group of trees overlooking a vast valley of green. There are sheep scattering the land as far as the eye can see. The sky is deep blue with white, fluffy clouds scattered throughout.

"So amazing," Eddie exclaims, "every time I see that, I'm still amazed."

"Yeah," Angela agrees, "pretty spectacular."

Advocate of Time   Craig Allan

"It amazes even me," Aganon interjects, "every single time. The power of God is an amazing thing."

"Sure is Ag buddy," Robbie agrees. "Shall we?" He asks, pointing the way.

"After you brother," Eddie says, gesturing to the doorway.

Robbie nods, "Okay, I'll go first this time." He turns toward the portal, looks to Aganon, and nods. Aganon nods in return. Robbie steps through the portal with his hand held up slightly in front of him. They see him step into the trees in the scene of the portal, then turn back toward them.

"Hey Ag," Robbie asks, "I can see the exact image of you all standing there watching me. Will that portal let me travel back the way I came?"

"Only one way to find out Robbie, come on back." Aganon suggests.

"Okay, here goes." Robbie says, walking back toward them. He steps through the portal and is standing with them again.

"Wow, totally cool," he exclaims. "It's about ten degrees warmer over there, let's go guys." Robbie says, and steps back into the portal again. They follow him closely. After the last one has gone through Aganon flicks his arm upward, pulling his lariat free. He wraps it up, hangs it back on his waist band, and steps through the portal. Once he is through the portal winks out of existence. The air swirls gently where the portal swims away, then the air is calm, and there is nothing.

Aganon turns toward the valley, taking in the vast green of the grazing lands. Eddie stands next to him, gazing at the beauty of the land of Midian.

"There must be thousands of sheep out there Ag." He says in amazement. "I don't think I've ever seen so many animals in one place in my entire life; and I've been to Texas where I've seen the sprawling lands filled with cattle. That was nothing compared to this."

Aganon nods in agreement. This is some sight to behold. They stand in awe for several minutes just taking in the view. Off in the distant east, on a hillside no less than two miles away, they see a small figure moving a group of sheep toward a small body of water. The figure is too far away to make out any detail, but they are all sure that it's Moses.

"Is that him Ag?" Becky asks, already knowing that it is.

"Yes it is," Aganon replies. "He's moving that small heard of sheep to early graze closer to their village.

He'll be coming this way. We'll wait here. It will give us some time to make a plan for the days to come."

"He's a ways off Ag," Joey says. "How long will it take him to reach us?"

"No less than four hours is my guess," He replies, a calculating look on his face, "depending on how long that herd waters, and how fast it moves across the valley."

"Could be as long as six hours," Eddie adds.

Aganon nods in agreement. They sit on the hillside watching the clouds move overhead, and enjoy the summer breeze. They watch as the sheep move back and forth along the valley. They see the figure moving across the distant valley, its approach slowed by the constant grazing of the sheep.

"That looks to be a very tedious job Ag," Laura suggests.

"What's that Laura?" He replies.

"Shepherding," She says.

"I imagine it is, never tried it myself, Moses seems to be fairly good at it though. I imagine it takes a mountain of patience, caring, and perseverance. All of which seemed to be lost on the Moses of the past. At least, that is how it appeared when we saw him as he was in the courts of the Pharaoh." Aganon considers. "I'm guessing that his time here in Midian has softened him, brought him closer to his readiness to accept Gods plan for his life."

"By now he probably has his family well established," Eddie adds. "He has been married for many years now, and is employed by Jethro, the priest of Midian."

"Will we see him speak to The Lord God in the burning bush Ag?" Angela asks, with fear in her voice.

"We will see Moses," Aganon replies sternly, "but we are not permitted to look on the bush where The Lords angel holds fire for The Lord God to speak to Moses. It is a holy place, and we will not be permitted to enter. The Lord will allow us to listen, and we must not speak, or make any sound. Do we all understand quite well?"

"Yes," Eddie says.

"Yeah," says Robbie.

"Yes," Angela replies.

"Sure," Laura replies.

"Yeah," Joey says.

"Oh yeah, we got it," Becky says, nodding solemnly.

"Very good," Aganon responds with strength in his voice. "Then we wait."

They continue to watch as Moses crosses the vast valley into the desert to the west. The small heard of sheep he shepherds moves steadily behind him as he leads.

"He will pass us to the south and will rest on that mount to the south," Aganon explains. "That evening, he will speak to The Lord of Hosts in a burning bush, that moment defining the rest of Moses' life as a prophet of God, and the leader of the Israelites." Aganon continues, "This area is known as Horeb, also Mount Sinai. It will later be known as a holy place, only after Moses speaks to God here. Right now, the region is just called Sinai."

They continue to await Moses arrival. As he approaches from the east, they can see that he has aged by many years and that he has softened. As Aganon has said, Moses and his heard pass them to the south. They cross into the desert, and take rest at the mount. Once the flock comes to rest, they set out to see Moses meet with The Lord. They are all nervous, but none feel any fear. They approach the heard of sheep from the east, the same direction Moses passed. As they approach his camp, they see him walking into the rocks with his staff. This is it! They follow him, but Aganon holds them back in a group of rocks that barely have a view of Moses. He is looking to the south where the desert continues to spread out for miles. As he turns back toward Aganon and his charge, his face is suddenly lit up a brilliant orange color and he is frozen in mid-stride, staring at the source of the glow. Suddenly, there is a rumbling in the ground and rocks that surround them. They huddle closely together, watching Moses, and not moving. Moses turns to look at the bush to see why it burns but is not consumed. When he does this, the Lord God calls to him

"Moses! Moses!" The Lord calls from the midst of the burning bush.

"Here I am." Moses says.

"Do not draw near this place." God tells him. "Take the sandals off your feet for the place where you stand is holy ground."

"I am the God of your father-the God of Abraham, the God of Isaac, the God of Jacob.

Then they saw Moses hide his face, he was afraid to look upon the Lord God.

Then God said to him, "I have surely seen the oppression of my people in Egypt, and have heard their cry because of their taskmasters, for I know their sorrows."

Advocate of Time   Craig Allan

Moses listened as God told him of his covenant with the children of Israel. God explained how he has heard their cries, how he will deliver them out of the hands of the Egyptians, and will give them a new land that flows with milk and honey. God tells Moses to go back to Egypt and deliver his people out of bondage. God tells Moses that the Pharaoh has died, and the charges against Moses died with him. That he is no longer a fugitive.

"I will send you to Pharaoh that you may bring My people, the children of Israel, out of Egypt." God says to Moses.

But Moses said to God, "Who am I that I should go to Pharaoh, and that I should bring the children of Israel out of Egypt?"

God continues to tell Moses that He will be with him and that He will guide him, and He will lead him so that the children of Israel will hear him, and will believe. Moses tells God that he is not a good speaker, and he cannot speak well to these people. God then gets angry and tells Moses that his brother Aaron is a good speaker, and will speak for Moses, and that Moses will be there to lead the people. God also explains to Moses that he will give Moses the ability to perform miraculous signs for Pharaoh so that he will believe that God has sent him, and that he must let My people go. Moses agrees to go back to Egypt with his brother Aaron and speak to Pharaoh. The Lord leaves the burning bush, and Moses goes back to his heard. He gathers them and prepares to go back to his father-in-law.

After Moses moves on, Aganon and his charge come out of the rocks. They are all visibly shaken. They have heard the true voice of God himself speaking to the prophet Moses. There has never been another experience like it their entire lives. They have been transformed.

Aganon gathers them together, and sits them down.

He speaks gently to them, "Nothing has changed my friends. We are still on a quest for enlightenment. You have heard the voice of your God, and you have accepted his command of Moses for what it is. There is nothing more than that to it. God allowed us to hear. Accept it for what it is, and allow us to move on."

They nod, and then join hands to pray to the Lord, and give thanks. When they have finished, Aganon outstretches his arm, pointing after Moses and his herd of sheep moving north toward Midian.

"He returns home to his wife, and to tell his father-in-law that he must return to Egypt. He will meet with his brother Aaron on his return to Egypt where he will explain to him what it is God has called them

90

to do. It is God's plan that Moses will return to Egypt as a representation of God himself, and Aaron will be his prophet to Pharaoh." Aganon pauses. He looks around the camp, and then continues. "Now we must decide where we will meet up with him next." Many things will take place in Moses' life from this moment on. He has been chosen by God, and his journey has begun."

Aganon falls silent. After a minute, he walks over to a tree that grows between two rocks. He looks at it, then at the large rock to his left. It appears he has chosen the next portal site.

"We have to choose our next destination guys." Eddie says. "What do we want to see next?"

"We know that Moses and Aaron will get the Israelites to accept their words, and the commandments of God. They will believe, and worship God." Angela offers for consideration. "So," she asks. "What about their meeting with Pharaoh? Is that where we want to go next?"
"Sounds good to me," Laura agrees.

"Yeah, I like it," Eddie says.

"Yeah," Robbie agrees also.

The others nod, and as quick as that, their next destination is chosen. They get up and walk over to Aganon. He turns toward them and asks,

"So you will see them make Gods command to Pharaoh." He says.

"You heard us then." Eddie offers.

"No," He replies, "but that is what I would do. Are we ready?"

"I think so, yes." Eddie says.

"Very well," Aganon replies. "Let's get this show on the road then."

Aganon tosses his lariat up and around the top of the small tree. He steps back, and climbs to the top of the large rock that stands a few feet from the tree. He squats down, closing the rope on the rock creating a doorway between the ground, the rock, and the tree. The portal begins to wink and a scene of a royal throne room begins to appear in the center of the doorway. Suddenly the scene winks into existence, and as if they are watching a movie screen, they see the throne room of Pharaoh. It is lined on all sides with tall pillars, and gold is inlayed in everything. The room is bright, and beautiful. They are nearly too amazed to even enter its presence. The one thing that helps them to move forward is the fact that they cannot be seen by anyone. Pharaoh sits in a throne of pure gold. He is a very dignified young man, who appears to look upward, while looking down with is eyes.

"Oh wow, he looks like a total snob," Angela says in disgust.

"Oh, you can rest assured that he is very much a snob Angela," Aganon confirms, "he looks down his nose at everything and everyone. He thinks of himself as god."

"I don't know if I can even be in the same room with him," Joey mentions in distaste, "he actually makes me sick."

"Remember Joey," Aganon encourages him, "technically, you are not in the room with him, just viewing from a different time."

"Yeah, okay," he agrees.

"Are we gonna do this or what?" Robbie asks impatiently.

"Ready when ya'll are," Laura says, the strength in her voice lifting their spirits.

"Here goes," Eddie says, and walks through the portal, holding Angela's hand, and drawing her along behind him. Laura follows them, grabbing Robbie by

the arm, pulling him behind her. Becky looks at
Aganon, and then into the portal, she grabs Joey's
hand pulling him along and walks in confidently, and
walks in confidently. Aganon stands up, jumps down
to the ground in front of the portal, and brings his
lariat back with the flick of his wrist. He looks back
toward the desert of Midian one last time, and walks
through. The scenes displays the seven of them all
looking up, and around; with their mouths hanging
open in awe of the glittering throne room. The portal
shimmers momentarily, and then winks out of
existence leaving a tiny dust devil in its wake. It spins
out as quickly as it started, then the air is calm once
again, and no evidence of their passing remains.

In the throne room of Pharaoh, Aganon and his
charge are taking in the splendor and majesty of this
luminous room filled with gold and jewels. The walls
are lined with paintings and drawings depicting
Pharaoh and his events. He is shown as an elevated
person, being worshiped and adorned as a god. The
room itself is vast, reaching great heights at its
ceiling, and having large pillars parading down a long
corridor that opens onto a courtyard. The courtyard
is decorated with sculptures; statues, and reliefs of
Pharaoh, many bodies of water in sculpted pools;
and trees of deep green, with lush green grass
growing between the stone walkways. The image is
like something right out of the movies. They stand in

awe, no one is able to speak, or even move. They hardly breathe. Finally someone speaks and breaks the silence.

"The Egyptians made all of this?" Laura says in awe and amazement.

"The Egyptians design it Laura, but it's the slaves that do the work. They are quite skilled." Aganon replies.

"It's all so beautiful, I can hardly describe it." She says.

"Yes, they were responsible for great works of art, and architecture." He replies.

"It's hard to imagine them doing all of this with hand tools, so many millenniums before power tools and technology." Eddie says in awe.

"The power of slavery," Angela replies, in quiet disgust.

"They were so into themselves, so arrogant." Becky reflects.

"Wait until you see the Romans." Aganon replies. "Talk about arrogance, and the worship of self. There is a perfect example."

"How is it that Moses will be able to come all the way into the inner palace and see Pharaoh?" Joey asks.

"He was wanted for a crime, and has been gone for over forty years. If I were the king, there's no way I would be able to find the time to see him."

"It is with great urging and persuasion that he finally gets his audience with Pharaoh, Joey." Aganon replies. "This meeting was months in the making. They were not accepted lightly. Aaron; who speaks for Moses, is a great speaker, and can be very convincing, as you well know from the scriptures."

They hear a murmur of voices, and a rush of hurried footfalls from the long corridor where Pharaoh sits on his throne. They turn to look, and see the people lining up in preparation for the arrival of this prophet from God. The word has already spread through Egypt that a man is coming to demand the release of all of Israel, and he claims to be sent by God himself. The one the nation of Israel call Yahweh, whom Moses will refer to as, I Am. The hall begins to slowly fill up with only the richest and most influential people of Egypt. They wish to see this man ask such a monumental thing of the king, and see him thrown out. Such things are of great interest to the curious depths of corrupt mankind. They see the royal procession taking their place among the throne of the king. Pharaoh will be the very last to make his appearance. The whole world, as he would like to think, shall wait for his coming. The high people of Egypt continued to pour into the hall so that there was barely a walkway down the middle of the pillar lined corridor where Moses would approach. Aganon and his charge began to make their way into the hall from the garden. They all knowingly glanced at each other, and then silently agreed on their direction. They started down the corridor, Eddie leading. Spread out to his left was Laura, Angela, and Joey, to his right was Becky and Robbie. Aganon followed closely behind. As they slowly walked up the corridor toward the throne of the king, they begin to get only the slightest idea of what it must have been like for Moses and his brother Aaron to approach the king with all of the people looking on. To be in the kings presence in the high court, to risk so much. In this place, there is nothing stopping the king and his soldiers from seizing and killing Moses and Aaron once they are within the city walls. Knowing this makes the walk up the corridor all the more ominous.

As they walk toward the throne, they glance at the people looking up at Pharaohs high seat, where his clergy of pagan enchanters and sorcerers await the arrival of God's holy man. They jeer, and mock. They whisper among themselves about what Pharaoh will do with this Moses and his brother.

Eddie notices a woman in the line of people at the side of the hall. She is adorned in such fine linens and jewelry that is seems amazing she can even stand.

The most amazing thing is that she is looking right at them as they pass. She is actually following their passing, but she appears to be dazed, almost sleeping. Eddie questions Aganon.

"Ag, that woman seems to be able to see us," Eddie says, with concern.

"Yes, I see her too Eddie, but I assure you, she cannot see us. What she is seeing is whatever daydream is playing in her mind, you can tell by her blank expression. Her subconscious person is aware of something going on in front of her, and she is following it without even knowing. It all returns to the human factor and what you are willing to cloud yourselves with."

He pauses to look at the woman again, "The inner; or core person; the one that seeks righteousness, still breathes and lives. It is that part of her that sees our passing. That woman seeks righteousness; she will turn to the Lord God soon in her life. She will forsake the life she has lived, and give herself to worship the true God; yet so few of these people will. His mercy endures forever. The events she will witness today will change her just watch and see"

As Aganon and his charge are halfway up the hall toward the throne, Pharaoh comes out and looks upon his people. He walks to his throne and his servants lift his long robes as he sits. After he is seated and in position, they lay the robes length across his waist and lap. He sits observing the gathering of people as they await the arrival of the God of Israel's prophet. Eddie almost stops in his tracks as Pharaoh looks right at them, right through them. Aganon tells them, "Fear not, he cannot see us. Most certainly a man in such depth of sin and idolatry cannot see the glory of God and his works."

They continue to within ten yards of the throne where they turn to take position in an archway that leads from the throne hall. As they turn to face Pharaoh and his court, they hear the hush fall over the crowd; and the rustle of hundreds of garments as they turn in unison to look to the end of the hall. Aganon and his charge look that way as well; they see the entryway to the corridors where the outer hall approaches the throne room. There, they see a young man, finely dressed, enter the hallway. Behind him follows two older men. One has a long staff and a full beard. His hair is also long, just past his shoulders. He is wearing shepherding garments and a robe, this man is Moses.

Next to him, younger in appearance, and much more neatly kept, is Aaron, Moses' brother. He is wearing Hebrew garments. The dress of a common man, but still well kept. His hair is cut, and his beard is trimmed short. He walks slightly ahead of Moses behind the boy who leads them.

They approach slowly, taking in the throne room, and its hall. All eyes follow them, their approach, and their passing. Nobody speaks, nobody moves. The only sound is the rustle of Moses robes and the tap of his staff as they progress toward Pharaoh. This is a true sight of a man who trusts in God, and does his will. Moses well knows that the Egyptians could capture him, and his brother Aaron. He knows they could be in grave danger, yet he performs the will of God. He is faithful, steadfast, obedient, and most importantly, he is willing to lay down his life for what God has asked of him. He does not look proud, nor does he show fear. He is merely a messenger sent to bring word from God, and he intends to do just that. These are two men chosen by God himself to carry a message of enormous weight to the king of the land. They come before Pharaoh with the power of God himself within them.

As they near the throne, Pharaoh's soldiers step out from the sentry area around the inner throne room and hold their spears across Aaron's path. Aaron and Moses stop where they stand.

"Come no closer prophets of the God of Israel," the Egyptian soldier commands.

Advocate of Time   Craig Allan

"Look upon me sentry," Aaron says, "I am no prophet, I merely speak on my brothers behalf, and we have word from God."

The soldier does not change his position or stance. Moses and Aaron wait where they are until they are summoned to approach Pharaoh.

One of Pharaohs advisors steps forward from his position near the throne and approaches Moses and Aaron.

"What have you to do with the almighty of Egypt this day?" He demands.

Aaron speaks, "We seek audience with Pharaoh in regard to the nation of Israel."

The pompous advisor looks at Pharaoh. Pharaoh motions for them to be allowed to approach. The soldier lifts his large spear to allow them to pass. They approach the throne of Pharaoh and Aaron speaks.

"Thus says the Lord God of Israel: 'Let My people go, that they may hold a feast to Me in the wilderness.'"

"Who is this Lord," Pharaoh Replies, "that I should obey His voice to let Israel go? I do not know the Lord, nor will I let Israel go."

"The God of the Hebrews has met with us. Please, let us go three days' journey into the desert and sacrifice to the Lord our God, lest He fall upon us with pestilence or with the sword."

"You arrogant Hebrews," Pharaoh says, getting angry. "Why do you take the people from their work? Get back to your labor! Look the people of the land is many now and you make them rest from their labor!"

With this, Pharaoh gets up and storms out of the throne room with his advisors and servants rushing behind him. The guards escort Moses and Aaron down the hall and out into the corridor. Aganon can see them leaving through the open doors. There begins to rise a heavy murmur among the people watching, and then they begin to leave the hall as well. Soon, the hall is empty again, and only Aganon and his charge are left there. Still looking on toward the hall and the corridor where Moses and Aaron went out.

Finally Laura speaks, "Well, that is not at all how I pictured the first meeting of Moses and Pharaoh as it reads in the scriptures." She says.

"Yeah," Angela agrees, "much different in person."

They nod in agreement. Aganon turns toward the corridor and points the way out with his outstretched arm. They walk down the hall toward the doors, and then out into the corridor. They have a long walk ahead of them. They are becoming aware that any time they are in the city; they have to make a long trip out of it so they can travel through portals. There are few God made objects left within the walls of Raamses.

As they are leaving the city Pharaoh is meeting with the Head taskmaster of the Israelites.

"Yes my eminence," the head taskmaster says to Pharaoh, "you summoned me my lord."

"Yes, I want you to make the work of the Hebrews harder." Pharaoh commands him. "They appear to have enough time on their hands to send a prophet of their God to request their release. Make sure they know that their suffering is due to their request to worship their God." He continues. "I want you to cease their supply of straw for their brick making. Tell them to get it themselves, and even though this will take them longer, their work load will not be reduced. Their daily quota will still be met, or their suffering will be as never before."

Pharaoh becomes violently angry as he speaks. "Let more work be laid on the men, that they may labor in it, and let them not regard false words." Pharaoh turns to leave, then looks back at the head taskmaster, "make them gather straw on their off time, let them gather it from outside the city. We will provide them with nothing." He says, then storms out of the room. The taskmaster considers his orders, then he to leaves the room. He has to pass his orders down, and he must get started right away. He wonders how one man could make Pharaoh so angry, so quickly. He is certainly glad he is not this Moses prophet. Pharaoh's wrath will be as never before if he continues with trying to get his people set free.

Chapter 8

Let my people go!

A light breeze stirs on the grass in the Pharaohs personal garden. All is silent in the city of Raamses. In neighboring Goshen the Israelites have been hard at their labors making brick with no straw. They have accused Moses and Aaron of making them appear abhorrent in the eyes of Pharaoh by requesting their release. Rather than blame Pharaoh for their captivity, they have blamed Moses. Moses has spoken with The Lord and He has promised him that Israel's deliverance is assured. Moses once again must return to Pharaoh and request that he set the children of Israel free.

As the breeze picks up across the garden outside the throne room, a ripple appears in the air near the pool of water farthest from the courtyard entrance. Suddenly, Angela and Laura hand in hand, pass through thin air into the garden; followed closely by Eddie, Robbie, Becky, and then Joey. Last, Aganon passes into existence pulling his whip behind him. The air stills where they passed through into the garden, then all is calm and quiet. They stand close together facing the throne room corridor as Aganon rolls up his whip and stows it away. They have come to see Moses meet with Pharaoh a second time.

The crowds are not as large as when they visited the first time. The people of Raamses have apparently seen all they care to, and now the passing of Moses into the sight of the king is old news. Just as the first time, Aganon and his charge slowly walk into the corridor and toward the throne of Pharaoh. They pass a few finely dressed Egyptians lined up along the pillars of the corridor. They do not notice the angel of time and the six young people passing within mere inches of where they stand. Aganon and his charge take the same position they had on their first visit. The Pharaohs guards are in place along the foot of the throne. The Pharaoh's court begins to enter the room and take place around the throne and inner room. After a long pause a deathly quiet settles over the crowd of people like a blanket.

All eyes turn as Pharaoh enters the room; he comes in through his inner chambers, pauses to look upon his subjects lined up in the corridor, and then slowly moves toward his throne. He sits down slowly, still observing with distrust the people present in the room. As Pharaoh sits and waits the arrival of yet another prophetic message, he continues to look upon his people. Not with love, caring, or pride, but with a contempt that appears all across his face like a mask. The King has a real hatred for the people whom serve him. The feeling is present upon him. They all feel this, and they are afraid for it.

Eddie notices the look on Pharaohs face and mentions to the others, "He looks like he'd rather have them all killed than sit in audience with them," Eddie says with sadness in his voice.

"He is a very frightened and angry man Eddie," Aganon replies. "He does not understand the true meaning of his throne, and the multitude of blessing The Lord God would permit him, if he only would obey God's law, and His word. Pharaoh is so obsessed with his power and his reign that he cannot see what it is he is truly meant for. What it is that God intends for him."

Aganon turns toward the far end of the corridor as he hears someone approaching. Eddie and the others follow his gaze. The doors swing open, and through them come a small group of people. In the lead is the same page boy who led them up to see Pharaoh on their last visit, this time they are also escorted by four guards. The appearance is of men in custody rather than prophets coming with a message from The Most High. They stop a few yards from the throne of the king. The guards take up position behind Moses and Aaron, appearing to block their path out the way they had come. Moses and Aaron are not bothered in the least by the display of Pharaohs guards. They know that God has sent them, and He will also make way their departure. The will of God will be done.

Aaron steps forward and speaks to Pharaoh once again,

"The Lord God commands that his people be released out of bondage in Egypt, and journey to the wilderness where they can make their offerings and prayers to Him."

"Who is this God you continue to speak of Aaron? You speak of Him as though I should fear and obey, and yet, I have seen nothing to prove to me and my courts that your God exists." Pharaoh toys with Aaron and Moses.

"The Lord God has offered you this day a sign." Aaron says, and he holds his staff before them so that they may see it very well, then he tosses it onto the floor before them. The staff comes to rest and sits still on the floor. Aganon and his charge look very closely at the staff lying on the floor. At first, it appears that they will see nothing at all. Suddenly, as if a brisk wind brushed alongside the staff, it moves. It rocks very slightly, then, as if it were made of a rubber, it begins to stretch out in length. The end nearest Aaron's feet begins to drawn into a point and the end nearest Pharaoh begins to swell and round at its tip. Then the staff begins to curve in several places in the middle. Then, as if it had been lying there the entire time, the staff changes into a snake. The people in the room gasp in amazement, even Eddie and the others are amazed. The staff transformed into a snake right in front of their eyes.

The serpent draws back slightly from the throne of Pharaoh and coils up in large coils in front of Aaron, as if it were guarding the prophetic men of God. Pharaoh, appearing to be unimpressed with this sign from God, motions to his wise men. They step forward, each with a staff in their hand. The three of them look on to Aaron and Moses, not looking at the serpent in front of them.

"Show them," Pharaoh says to his magicians.

The three magicians throw their staves down in front of themselves and each one begins to shape shift as it bounces on the floor. One at a time, the staves become snakes, and they each take up an aggressive position in front of the serpent of Aaron's staff. Pharaoh laughs loudly,

"What of your miracles now? Oh prophet of The Most High God" Pharaoh mocks. "Your staff has become a serpent and yet so have mine, you have shown me nothing."

As Pharaoh is speaking, the Aaron's staff snake lifts its head high above the three snakes of the magicians. It lunges forward in one swift motion and coils around the tree snakes, wrapping them up as one. The serpent then opens its mouth wide, and one at a time, it swallows the snakes whole. The three magicians step back in fear of the serpent, for they had thought their magic to be much more powerful than the magic of the God of these prophets. Pharaoh looks on in amazement, and then his amazement turns to fury as he begins to realize that his magic has been destroyed by the power of God.

"This magic trick means nothing to me Moses," Pharaoh fumes in anger.

"I ask you for the last time Pharaoh, let my people go," Moses says in a gentle and commanding tone.

Eddie looks at Aganon; the others stare in awe and amazement. Aganon smiles and looks back to Moses.

"If you do not do as The Lord commands Pharaoh, the suffering on Egypt will be as never seen before," Aaron assures Pharaoh.

"I will not let the Hebrews go!" Pharaoh shouts at them. "The more you demand it, the more I will swell their suffering. That is one prophecy you can be assured will come to pass."

"Your hardened heart has assured your own destruction Pharaoh. There will be ten plagues upon the land of Egypt. The Lord God has spoken, and it shall come to pass." Aaron says to Pharaoh in sadness. Aaron bends down to pick up the serpent at his feet, and as he reaches for it, the people in the throne room gasp in unison as he grasps it, and it becomes his staff once again.

Aaron and Moses turn to leave, and without Pharaoh having to command them, the guards part to allow the prophets to go their own way. Pharaoh watches in fury as they slowly walk out of his sight. He is so furious he forgets that his magicians and his guards have failed him; and let the only two men whom have ever humiliated him walk right out of his presence, and they did nothing. When he finally realizes they are gone, and his guards let them go, he sends them all to the farthest reaches of Egypt to work in the slave camps. The magicians are sent away, never to return or be put to death.

Aganon and his charge follow Moses and Aaron out of the city. They watch in amazement as the prophets of God are allowed to walk all the way out of the city, without so much as a jeer or a bit of trouble from any of the Egyptians.

"Only by the grace of God," Robbie says in a whisper.

"These men are surely under the divine protection of God," Eddie replies.

"Indeed they are," Aganon agrees.

"What will happen now, Ag?" Laura asks.

"Well, in a few days," Aganon says, "Moses will release upon the land the first of the ten plagues. He will turn the river to blood, and Aaron will turn the remaining water in the land to blood. This will be the beginning of the horrible wrath of God upon all of Egypt." He pauses to allow them to give the events to follow some thought, and he continues.

"Will we be there to see it happen?" He asks them as a group.

They look one to another; at first nobody responds and then one at a time they nod in agreement to each other, then to Aganon.

"It is settled then," Aganon says. "Tomorrow, we shall witness one of Moses greatest acts of God; the turning of all the water in Egypt to blood. We have a big day ahead of us; let's go to our hillside for some food and rest."

Aganon turns and walks toward the hillside where they make their camp, and his charge follows him. As they leave the city, Moses and Aaron are leaving in the opposite direction to find their holy place where they can have counsel with God.

As they walk up the street toward their hillside camp Becky asks,

"Ag, when Moses spoke to Pharaoh today, everyone was surprised. Why?"

"Eddie?" Aganon passes the question to Eddie.

"The word of God says that God made Moses like himself," Eddie explains, "and made Aaron to be a prophet to Moses. There is no real documentation aside from the written word of God about who actually did the speaking to Pharaoh during their meetings. It was widely accepted that Aaron did all of God's speaking for Moses, and that Moses was simply the shepherd that led them. Today, we actually saw Moses speak to Pharaoh. There are a lot of things that happened in the days of the bible that were simply not written. I think we witnessed one of them today." Eddie concludes, looking at Aganon.

"That's right Eddie, the word of God is not a complete, word for word account of all that happened in these times, but it tells the greater part of the story, so much is still left unsaid, and that is the beauty of this assignment, this charge. We will see, and hear a great deal of what has been left unsaid. We are very blessed with God's grace in this endeavor. We should not take it lightly." Aganon says.

"We won't," Angela replies. The others nod in agreement.

"We learn more and more every moment we are here," Joey says, "how blessed we are to be allowed such a miracle from God. We are very thankful."

They approach the hillside, and Aganon turns back toward town.

"I will go, and bring some food and refreshments." He says. "You all can get comfortable, and prepare for our evening. I shall return shortly."

Aganon walks back down the street the way they had come, and then disappears around the corner of a building. The others walk up the hillside and settle in around the house they had used the night before. Eddie makes a small fire, and they gather around and share with each other the events of the day, and what they felt at each moment. They all join hands and pray to God for strength, and understanding in the days to come. They each say a fervent and reverent prayer, and then close with a shower of thanksgiving for their many blessings, and gifts. They thank The Lord for everything. As they sit in the afterglow of God's presence, Aganon comes up the hillside with a pack of food and drink. He has also brought along some blankets, and a bucket of water.

"Howdy Ag, you just missed our prayer meeting," Becky says, "It was great."

"I didn't miss it Becky," he replies, "I'm a part of everything you all do that goes to God. He makes sure that I get enough prayer coverage to make our journey possible, and to keep us all in the same Godly mind set."

"I don't understand what you mean Ag," Laura says.

"Prayer is what gives angels their strength Laura," he replies, "that's how we work God's miracles. We not only draw our power from God, but from the prayers of His people. In my case, I draw directly from my charge."

"Wow," Joey interjects, "so the more we pray to God for our quest, or for you directly, the more power you will receive?"

"Well," Aganon replies, "it's a little bit like that. I draw only what I need, but yes, your prayers for our quest, power our quest. It's a direct link to God's will."

"God is good..." Eddie says.

"...All the time," the others say in unison.

"And all the time..." Angela echoes.

"...God is good." Eddie and the others echo in unison.

"Amen," Aganon says, and hands the pack of food to Eddie. Eddie looks inside, pulls out a small loaf of bread, and a piece of fruit, and passes the pack on to Laura. The pack goes around to everyone, and they pray over their food. They pray for guidance, and direction in their quest, they pray for Aganon to have God's divine strength to lead them where they need to go, and they pray for God's protection on them all. They close their blessing by thanking God for all He has done in each of their lives, and they thank Him for bringing them Aganon. They all say Amen. Aganon, smiling bright and wide, raises his hands to them all and says, "Let's eat," and they do.

They talk of their day, the days to come, the mysteries of God's miracle of them traveling through time, and the miracle of their own time at home standing still for them. After they have finished eating, and they have run out of things to talk about, they turn in one at a time. Aganon is finally left tending the fire, and watching the city as it quietly passes to sleep, and prepares for the next day. He thinks to himself, they have no idea of the things to come.

"Things sure do appear to be going very well in your quest," a gentle voice speaks from outside the fire light.

"His glory, His name," Aganon greets his visitor as he comes into the light.

"His name, His glory," Percival greets Aganon in return.

"What brings you this far out Percy?" Aganon asks.

"Just doing my job Ag, you know how it is." Percival replies.

"Sure," Aganon replies, "Did you follow through my portal?"

"Yeah, but don't worry," Percival says, "The Almighty Himself opens and closes the portal once you have gone, It is not passable except by way of Him whom sent us. He is just allowing me to see how they are. They are my charge as well you know."

"Of course," Aganon agrees. "How are things in Webster?"

"Boring, that's why I'm here.

They look at each other for a moment, and then laugh quietly.

"Yes, I imagine without the six of them to keep you running, you might get to the point of nodding off." Aganon jokes.

"Oh yes, you can say that again," Percy agrees, "these are good kids, and very righteous as well, but they still keep me on my toes, after all, they are kids."

"True enough,"

"Have they given you any trouble at all?" Percy asks.

"Not a bit. They were all shaken when they saw Moses kill a man, but they managed it just fine. They know why they are here."

Percival nods. They sit side by side in silence for a moment.

"Are you staying?" Aganon says, breaking the silence.

"Would that interfere with your charge?" Percival asks.

"That depends on your desire to be seen or unseen." Aganon replies.

"Oh, this is enough for them;" Percival says, "I'll stay out of sight, most certainly. I would feel better if I could be involved in what they are doing, rather than sitting around back home, when they are not around. You know what I mean Ag?"

"Of course I do Percy," Aganon says, gently grasping his shoulder, "you are most welcome to stay."

"Thanks Ag, you are truly a servant of The Most High," Percy replies with joy.

"The more, the merrier Percy," Aganon says with a chuckle.

"Strength in numbers," Percy says.

"Indeed," Aganon agrees, "strength in numbers."

The two angels sit together around the dwindling fire and take in the sight of the city of Raamses. It almost looks peaceful on its last night before the onslaught of Gods wrath. Their lives will forever be changed.

Chapter 9

Waters turn to blood

Angela is the first to awaken. The new day is barely dawning, and the light is not quite settled on the land. She steps out of the building they have called home for the last two nights. She sees Aganon sitting next to a very small fire.

Aganon notices her, and he flashes his winning smile. Angela smiles back, walking toward the fire. As she approaches the fire she hears someone yawn behind her, she turns and sees Joey coming out of the house followed by Becky and Eddie.

"Looks like the gang is coming alive Ag," Angela says playfully.

"Yes ma'am," Aganon replies in a southern drawl.

"You make me laugh when you talk like that Aggie," She says, and she bats his hat down in the front, covering his face slightly. She laughs. Aganon laughs with her.

Advocate of Time   Craig Allan

"What's going on over here? It's too early for comedy isn't it?" Becky says in a playful tone.

"It's never too early to have a good time," Joey says, following closely behind her.

"Looks like we have a couple of stragglers," Aganon says, nodding toward the house.

"Yep, Robbie and Laura have always been the last to rise," Eddie says.

"We'll need to run them out of there if they don't come along soon; we have a big day ahead." Aganon kindly suggests.

"I'm sure they'll be along shortly," Eddie suggests.

"Let's get breakfast on, that will speed things up a bit. How did everyone sleep?" Aganon asks them.

"Great," Eddie says.

"Yeah, the air here is so clean, and fresh, makes for a great nights rest," Angela agrees.

"Yep, slept like a log here," Joey adds.

"Yeah, slept great," Becky says.

Aganon nods, and then reaches behind him for a pack of food. He sets the pack in front of him.

Advocate of Time   Craig Allan

"We will wait for the others awhile longer," He says.

"You don't sleep either, do you Ag?" Becky suddenly asks.

Surprised by the sudden direct question; Aganon smiles and says,

"No Becky, I do not sleep. Does that bother you?"

"No, no. Not at all, just making verbal observations Ag," She says.

Eddie glances at Becky; she looks at him and shrugs. Someone begins to stir in the house where they slept.

Then Laura comes slowly into the new light of the day from inside the house, she stretches her arms toward the sky and says, "Praise God for this wonderful place, I have not slept this well in years," She says.

Robbie walks past her, puts his hand on her shoulder as he passes saying, "Make way sleeping beauty, some of us have food in mind."

"After you sir," She says sarcastically.

Robbie smiles making his way up the hill to the others, Laura follows closely behind.

"How did you two sleep?" Aganon asks.

"Oh Ag, it is so restful here, I slept like a rock," Laura replies.

"Same here, I feel great," Robbie adds.

"Great, there's some food here, we should get breakfast out of the way so we can play the events of our day, it's going to be a big one," Aganon says.

Laura sits down next to Angela, and Robbie takes a spot next to Becky and Joey across the fire. Aganon throws a couple pieces of wood on the fire, picks up the pack, and hands it to Eddie. He roots around in it for a few moments, takes out a small loaf of bread and a piece of fruit then passes the pack to Angela. She reaches in and takes out what she wants and passes to the next person. The pack makes its way around the fire, and ends up at Aganon's feet. He waits as they eat. They silently look around at the new day and consider the events that will unfold in the hours ahead.

Eddie finishes his food first, and he sits silently looking into the fire as the sky continues to brighten in the east.

"Ag," Eddie muses, "We are going to see the miracle of water turned to blood today, aren't we?"

Aganon just nods in response.

"Are we going to see all ten of the plagues of Egypt?" He asks.

"Do you want to?" Aganon replies.

Eddie looks at the others; they have all finished their breakfast and are looking at him. They slowly nod in agreement, as if casting a unanimous vote.

"I think we do Ag." Eddie finally answers.

"Then you shall," Aganon replies.

They sit silently for a few moments longer, just staring at the fire. Robbie finally gets up and goes off toward the house they now call their home.

"I think Robbie has the right idea," Aganon says. "The rest of you should prepare as well; we'll have to be leaving soon."

"Sure," Eddie says, getting up. He moves slowly toward their house. The others follow. Aganon smothers the fire with dirt as he waits for them to return. One at a time, they come back to the fire pit and sit down, waiting for the others. Once they are all gathered, they look at Aganon, indicating they are ready.

"Very well," Aganon finally says. "Let's get this show on the road."

Aganon stands up and pulls out his lariat. He turns to the rock outcropping he has been using. He twirls his rope in the air then tosses it around the tip of the rock outcropping creating doorway. The portal swirls and wavers into existence. This one to a few days in the future where the river Nile will run with blood and the Egyptians will watch in awe and horror as the waters of the entire land of Egypt are turned to blood; every last drop. They all pass through the portal with Aganon in rear as always. The portal winks out and only stillness is left.

Aganon walks slowly along the street at the edge of town as the children of Israel gather near the river banks outside the palace. Moses has stepped up to the water's edge. He is watching Pharaoh basking in the morning sun on his flat boat. Moses continues to stare at Pharaoh, watching his boats and his court approach. Pharaoh notices Moses standing at the river's edge, and watches him as he approaches.

Suddenly, Moses strides out into the water and raises his staff toward Pharaoh. Pharaoh motions his slaves to stop rowing to slow and listen to the crazed prophet. When Pharaohs boat stops Moses takes one more step closer, he looks directly at Pharaoh and says, 'The Lord God of the Hebrews has sent me to you, saying, "Let my people go, that they may serve Me in the wilderness." But instead, until now, you would not hear! Thus says the Lord, "By this you shall know that I am the Lord. Behold, I will strike the waters which are in the river with the rod that is in my hand, and they shall be turned to blood."' With that, Moses struck down with his staff into the water. The water rippled away from the staff, as Moses held Pharaohs stare.

Eddie looks at Aganon, Aganon's eyes are fixed on the scene unfolding before them. Nobody moves, or even breathes. It seems the whole world is standing still.

Pharaoh looks upon the prophet of the God of the Hebrews. He sees the display and hears his warning, yet, nothing has happened. Pharaoh starts to rise from his lofty chair to scoff at Moses, when suddenly, a ripple pulses through the water starting at the point where the staff enters. Pharaoh watches closely. Moses does not move, nor does he take his gaze from Pharaoh.

Then in a sudden splash of deep crimson, the water surrounding Moses' staff begins to grow red. In tendrils of the deepest red, the blood reaches outward toward the flowing river. The crimson wake quickly engulfs Pharaoh's boat, and then swallows up the entire river; north to south, and east to west. In a moment, the entire Nile River is flowing deep red, the color of freshly spilled blood. Moses backs out of the bloody flow slowly, and not a drop of blood is on him, or his robes. Pharaoh gazes in disbelief.

There he sits, on a royal boat floating in a river of flowing blood. He commanded his servants to get him back to the palace immediately. In the palace, Pharaoh summons his magicians and explains to them what he has seen in the river. His closest mystics assured Pharaoh it was nothing more than a magic trick. To prove this, they turned a cup of water to deep red, appearing to be the exact trick that Moses had apparently used on the river. This eases Pharaoh's mind, and keeps his heart hardened toward the Hebrews, Moses, and their God. What Pharaohs magicians did not tell him, is that at the very moment Moses turned the river to blood, his brother Aaron had waved his staff over the land of Egypt, and turned every single body of water in the land to blood as well, including cups, vases, buckets and puddles of water. There was not a drop of water in the land of Egypt that was not turned to blood, with one exception; the children of Israel. Their water supply was not harmed; they had all the water they would need.

Aganon and his charge stand at the water's edge, amazing at the miracle of God they had witnessed. Laura is trembling while Joey holds her, offering support to her and comforting himself as well. Eddie stares at the blood river, unable to speak, or move. Angela is by his side; Joey and Becky are behind them, they are staring at the blood river in the distance.

"Ag, have you ever seen this miracle of the first of ten plagues before?" Joey asks.

"Yes Joey," Aganon replies. They all look at him, "I was here when this happened; I was fighting the dark forces with the rest of the ranks of God's warriors." Aganon pauses. "Moses was guarded by countless numbers of heavenly warriors, at God's command. He was under constant attack by the enemy."

"Wow," Joey exclaims. "You were a warrior?"

"Sure," Aganon replies, "We all are; this is just a side job for me, and a great one at that. This charge has been my best ever."

"Thanks Ag," Eddie says, bewildered.

As they walk back down the street talking with each other, Moses walks through the city to his meeting place with God. Aaron follows close behind him. Angela looks back and sees him going up the hill.

"Ag," Angela says, "Moses and Aaron are leaving. Is this the part where they meet with God again, and he tells them that Pharaohs heart is hardened?"

"Yes Angela, Aganon replies. "This blood will last a week, as it is written. The Egyptians will dig wells near the rivers to gather fresh water. In a week, Moses will return to Pharaoh, but Pharaoh will turn him away."

"Let's go see what happens," Robbie says.

"Very well," Aganon says, "Back to the hillside."

They walk side by side, talking about what they have witnessed. As they make their way toward the hillside, the people of the city begin to moan and cry, for they cannot find any water anywhere. As the people begin to leave the river bank, the fish start to float to the surface and wash ashore. They are dying by the thousands. The stench will be like nothing the city of Raamses has ever beheld.

On the hillside, Aganon and his charge stand before the portal Aganon has opened. One at a time they walk through to the next meeting of Moses and Pharaoh.

They hurry out of the garden into the throne room and stand in their usual spot. Eddie stands at the foot of the throne, amazed at the sight of such an ornate and sculpted object, used to sit upon.

Laura whispers to him, startling him out of his study.

"Eddie," she whispers, "come on, he's coming."

Eddie quickly walks back to them, waiting for Pharaoh and Moses to meet once more.

"That chair is one big fat work of art, and treasure," Eddie says in amazement, "and it's only used for him to sit on, how arrogant." The chamber doors open at the end of the hall, and the young man leads Moses and Aaron down the long corridor toward the throne of Pharaoh. As they approach, Pharaoh enters the room, sits at his throne, and awaits Moses and Aaron.

"Which meeting is this Ag?" Robbie asks.

"This is during the plague of frogs." He replies.

"The frogs are here? Covering the land of Egypt? We gotta see that!" He sighs.

"Trust me Robbie," Aganon replies, "that is not an event you want any part in."

"Oh, yeah, right, pretty nasty. I read about it," he says.

Advocate of Time   Craig Allan

Moses approaches the throne and stops short of the steps.

"You sent for The Lords servants, Pharaoh?" He says.

"Entreat the Lord that He may take away the frogs from my land and from my people; and I will let His people go, that they may sacrifice to the Lord."

"Accept the honor of saying when I shall intercede for you, for your servants, and for your people, to destroy the frogs from you and your houses, that they may remain in the river only." Moses replies.

"Tomorrow," Pharaoh responds.

"Let it be according to your word, that you may know that there is no one like the Lord our God. And the frogs shall depart from you, from your houses, from your servants, and from your people. They shall remain in the river only."

Moses and Aaron turn from Pharaoh and leave the throne room. Pharaoh hangs his head in shame. His magicians had failed to take away the frogs, in fact, had added to them in their attempt to disprove Gods wonders. Pharaoh has been shown that God alone has the power to work great wonders and miracles.

"He's not even close to letting them go," Becky says, "this is where he goes back on his word with Moses, and with God the first of many times."

"He is earnestly intent on letting them go Becky," Eddie says, "but as soon as The Lord removes the frogs, and there is relief in the land of Egypt, he will change his mind and go back on his word."

"Coward," Robbie says, under his breath.

"Let's get back to the hillside," Aganon says, "we have to go through the streets of the city, and there are frogs everywhere. We don't want to be caught out there in the dark."

"Can't you just make us a portal to the hillside Ag?" Becky asks. "Walking through frogs doesn't sound like fun to me."

"No manmade object can support a portal," Aganon replies.

"Oh yeah," she says.

"Don't worry," he says, "they have kept the streets clear for the most part.

They leave the throne room with Pharaoh still seated at his throne with his head hung in shame. They make their way slowly through the palace and out to the streets. They see soldiers, Egyptian workers, and some Hebrew slaves with rakes and shovels, pushing the piles of live frogs back from the palace. Frogs are jumping, and squirming everywhere they look. There are frogs on tops of the houses; they are pouring out the windows and doorways, frogs have caused the marketplace to be shut down. They cover the merchant tables, jumping in and out of the vases and pots. Frogs are everywhere.

"These frogs where brought right from the rivers and the ground itself," Angela says, "The scriptures say that God did not create more frogs, but called them forth from the earth and the river. It's so amazing that there would be this many of them."

"Yeah," Joey says, "it seems impossible."

As the workers keep the streets as clear as they can, the travelers make their way through the inner city toward the outskirts of town. Once in awhile a frog or two will make its way in front of them, or will hop across their feet. Once, Becky squealed as a frog hopped over her foot, but she bravely pressed on. They finally make it through to the outside of town. They stop and stare back at the inner city where the frogs shine and glisten in the sun. In the distance near palace, the ground looks greenish brown, and shiny; with the appearance of moving like waves on the sea.

"Unbelievable," Eddie says with a sigh then continues to speak, "to think that this could have been avoided if only Pharaoh would have obeyed God."

"A great many things could be avoided," Aganon adds, "by all of mankind's obedience to The Lord God on High."

"True enough Ag," Eddie replies."

They turn away from the sight of the inner city, where the Egyptians battle back the wave of frogs. They find their portal tree and Aganon opens a portal back to Goshen and one at a time they gladly leave the frog infested city of Raamses.

They sit on the hillside near their preferred location to travel from, the rock outcroppings. Aganon sits hunkered on top of the large rock that juts straight up from the hillside. He looks like a large bird, resting on its perch. The others are gathered around beneath him, discussing where they will go next.

"So let's recap," Angela says. "We saw the first plague, the river and waters turned to blood. Then we saw the frogs today, it has been a week since the river was turned, now it's back to normal. The book of Exodus says the waters were blood for one week. So we are on track so far. The frogs will all die tomorrow, according to scripture, and the stench will be awful, not looking forward to that. Let's hope we have gone by then."

"The frogs were due to the refusal of Pharaoh to let God's people go after the first plague," Eddie adds. "So the frogs filled the land of Egypt, and Pharaoh had no choice but to call Moses and Aaron; not his magicians, to rid of the frogs. Moses even secures the fact that our God alone will perform this task, by having Pharaoh pick the time when they will be delivered from the frogs."

"Right; and now," Joey adds, "Pharaoh has remorse for not believing in the Lord God, but his heart will once again be hardened when the frog plague is lifted, and he will go back on his word. He will not let God's people go after all.

"Well," Becky chimes in, "I don't know about you guys, but I know what the next four plagues are, and it sounds disgusting to me. Third are lice, fourth are flies, fifth is diseased animals, and sixth is boils on the animals and the people. I have no desire whatsoever to see any of that. Do you?" She concludes, looking around at all of her friends.

"No," Robbie speaks up for the first time all day, "I don't care to see any of that."

"Me either," Laura agrees.

"That leaves the seventh plague; hail like Egypt has never seen before." Eddie adds.

"Right," Angela agrees, "I'm ok with that one, what about the rest of you?"

They consider what they know about this plague and they all agree.

"So I guess that's it then," Laura concludes, "We are off to witness the hail. Will we go to see Moses speak to Pharaoh again?"

"This time we will find Moses speaking to Pharaoh as he travels within the inner city. I don't think Moses and Aaron will be welcome in the palace anymore." Eddie says.

"So from here on," Robbie adds, "Moses will find Pharaoh in different places along him normal wanderings, and will speak God's will to him."

"Yep," Eddie agrees, "That's what I gather from the writings of the book of Exodus."

"I think we are ready Ag," Eddie says, looking up toward Aganon on his perch. Aganon is not there. Eddie looks on all the rock outcroppings; nothing. Aganon is gone.

"Ag!" Eddie yells out, wondering where the angel went.

Advocate of Time   Craig Allan

"Where is he?" Angela asks, sounding a little sheepish.

"I dunno," Eddie shrugs.

"There he is!" Joey says, pointing down the hillside toward the street.

They all look, and see Aganon coming down the street and toward the hill with two packs. He has gone for food again.

Aganon approaches them and asks, "You guys come up with a plan then?"

"Where did you go Ag? We almost got worried there," Eddie says, a little angry.

"What? You couldn't possibly think I left you," He replies. "I went for some food; you guys need to eat before we head out again. I wouldn't just run off on ya'll, you know that."

"Right, but usually, we let each other know when we are taking off, or heading out alone, and so on. Ya know?" Eddie adds.

"I had no idea, forgive me if I startled you. All of you, I'm sorry." He sadly replies.

"It's nothing Ag, we are just in a strange place, and you are our ride, ya know what I mean?" Robbie says.

"Right, I understand," He says.

"Hey, don't feel bad Ag," Angela adds, "We are the ones who are at fault here. As a human race, we are used to people leaving us, and letting us down. Angels don't have to deal with that sort of thing. So when we see you are not where you once were, we assume you have gone away, and won't return. You on the other hand, would assume we have gone to do something, and will be back shortly, with no doubts."

"Yes," Aganon replies.

"We are a flawed creature," Eddie adds.

"Humans are beautiful, you make such astounding music to worship The Lord," Aganon says. "Yours is the most high of all creatures under God. You may be flawed Eddie, but you are all loved so completely by God, that he will never forsake you. The blood of the Lamb has made you wonderful. Blessings are upon you all."

"Wow, thanks Ag," Angela says in awe.

They all sit staring at Aganon. They have never before heard such utter praise coming from anyone about them. They feel closeness to Aganon second only to God himself.

"You are beautiful to us Ag," Laura says, with tears in her eyes.

"Very much so," Eddie adds.

"Thank you my friends," Aganon says, "your love lifts me and gives me strength."

"Here is your lunch," Aganon says, handing one pack to Laura and the other to Robbie. "Have your rest and nourishment, then we will travel.

"We would like to see the Moses call down the hail," Eddie says.

"I thought you would," Aganon says, "the others are to vile to witness, as is the final plague. The tenth plague is one the hardest lessons a nation have experienced in all of God's creation. This is where the Passover begins."

"We haven't even discussed that one yet," Angela says, cringing.

"There is time," Aganon says.

Chapter 10

The Plagues

The traveling band of prayer warriors gather around the fire pit, eating their lunch. Traveling companions hardly notice the bright noon sky. They are deep in thought and prayer in preparation for their next group of events. They will travel to a plague that will cost thousands their lives. The events are written, and have taken place in their minds, thousands of years ago, yet, they will witness the power of God Almighty once more, and in person. They fear the event itself and for good reason. Few in history have witnessed God's mighty works and have gathered the grace and wisdom to tell of them. These will teach and preach of the things they have seen and what they have learned.

Eddie stands up and stretches his arms upward and leans back a bit in a full stretch. He turns toward the distant horizon overlooking the city. He stands there silent for a moment then speaks with his back turned to them.

"I feel as though we have grown so much since we have been here. I am scared stiff about where we are going next, but at the same time I am excited to grow closer to the scriptures," He pauses, "is that weird Ag?"

"Why would it be Eddie," Aganon says, "You have experienced history in the making. It's not weird that you want to continue to experience the events that you have studied for so long. Your fear is a result of what your mind created in relation to what you read. I think that is a natural response, however, you should not let your fear take control."

Eddie nods, saying "I know what you say is true, and I know my fears very well. I just don't know what to think about what we will see."

"None of us do Eddie," Laura adds.

"Yeah," Joey says, "Don't worry Eddie; we'll make it through, together."

"I'm not worried guys," Eddie says, a touch of pride showing in his voice, "I'm just bringing up some points to consider, that's all."

"We know Eddie," Laura says. She stands up and puts her hand on Eddies shoulder. "We have all been thinking a lot about where we are going."

"Speaking of where we're going," Robbie says as he stands up, "we should probably get a move on, don't ya think?"

"You say true Robbie," Aganon replies, "no better time than the present." He turns toward the rock they have used so many times to cast his portal in time.

"Let's have a word of prayer before we go," Eddie says.

"Yeah, good idea Eddie," Laura agrees. They gather together around the spent fire pit and put their arms around each other in a group embrace. Eddie leads the reverent address to the Lord and each of them say a bit of what is on their heart. They pray in honesty and faith. Aganon watches for a full minute, embracing the power that flows all around them. As he embraces the presence of The Almighty all around his charge he begins to gently weep. Such a rare find are these children of God. If there were only more like them, the world might be a different place. As they finish up their prayer Aganon turns back to his work. This portal must be exact. He cannot be out of alignment with the passages of time in the least bit.

He draws out his lariat, fashions a loop and begins to twirl it over his head. As the loop passes over his head he feeds out more and more until the loop is larger than he is. As the loop comes around past his head he gives a flick of his wrist and sends it sailing for the very top of the rock outcropping. It lands perfectly and with a quick backlash pull he tightens the slack in the rope. He walks across the lower part of the cleft in the rock and climbs across to the opposite side of the rock he has roped. As his feet come to rest on the peak of the rock opposite the cleft, the portal begins to spin into existence below him. As the portal completes its rotation it stills and wavers into a view of the city of Raamses from the garden of Pharaohs palace.

"If ya'll are ready," Aganon says, "We can head out anytime."

"Like you said Aggie," Joey jokes, "no better time than the present."

Joey slaps Eddies back and walks up to the portal, he glances back at his friends, then up at Aganon and he winks. Then without another moment spent he walks through the portal. The others watch for a moment then one at a time they walk to the portal. Becky is the next one to go through.

Eddie steps toward the wavering, purplish body of energy. As he is about to step through Aganon glances down at him. Suddenly, Aganon loses his footing and slips off the rock. He stumbles but catches his footing. But his foot has left the connection where the rope settles the portal and it begins to wink and flicker. Aganon flashes his hand toward Eddie.

"Eddie! Get back!" He says in a thundering, but gentle voice.

Before Aganon can turn back toward his waning portal, a flash of light penetrates their quiet circle and blasts through the flattening portal. Suddenly Joey and Becky stumble backward through the fading purple portal and then it winks out.

They fall onto their backs, shaken and dazed. Joey scrambles to his feet and blurts out.

 "What was that?"

"Yeah," Becky says still dazed, "it felt like we were just thrown from a moving truck."

Aganon looks past his charge to Percival who stands a few feet behind them.

"Thank you my old friend," Aganon says, nodding to Percival.

"You are most welcome Aganon," Percival replies, "just doing my job."

"Must have been a strong dark warrior to be able to push me off of my footing," Aganon says.

"The battle is always raging my friend," Percival says, "sometimes the lines get broken. One of them got through just long enough to get you off center, it has been dispatched. I apologize for the interruption." Percival says bowing his head slightly.

Eddie and his friends step back toward the fire pit and watch the exchange between Aganon and this new adventurer in their group. Their faces are blank and confused.

Aganon glances at them and stops his exchange with Percival,

"Tarnation! My manners," he says stepping down as he pulls his lariat up and off the rock in one fluid motion. He rolls it up and stows it as he reaches out to his charge.

"I am so sorry; I got caught in the moment and forgot to make your introductions," Aganon says; a little embarrassed.

"Percy, or Percival rather, needs no introduction of y'all, he knows you very well," Aganon says gesturing to Percival.

Advocate of Time   Craig Allan

"Eddie, Robbie, Laura, Angela, Becky, and Joey,"
Aganon says gesturing toward them, "this is Percival.
He is the soldier of the watch for your group events."

"He's in charge of the body of protection for the lot
of you when you are together as a group in Christ."
He pauses for them to absorb what he has said so
far. "His job is to make sure that each of your
personal guardian angels and your events are
provided for."

"What do you mean personal guardian angels Ag?"
Robbie asks.

"Uh, yeah, and what exactly is a soldier of the
watch?" Angela asks.

"They are a little surprised Ag," Percival says. "Let me
try to explain Ag."

"Sure thing Percy," Aganon nods.

"Ok, let me try to sum this up as best I can. Number
one, this was of course, not supposed to happen, but
the battle was fierce, I had to step in, that's why I'm
here; so we'll make the best of it."

"Each of you has a guardian angel to watch over you,
been there since your birth. Of course, that angel is
restricted from a great deal of involvement in your
lives up until you become one of God's chosen. After

you welcomed Jesus into your lives, they were given more latitude to work as participants rather than observers. Once the six of you found each other you created your charge; I'm sure Aganon explained to you about your charge, but I'll do what I can to add to it. You are chosen as a group, by God himself, to have a special relationship with each other, and with God. You also have access to certain aspects of the history of God and his people. That's what it means to be His charge. You are also Aganon's charge, because it is his job to provide your access to God's history. It is my job, to oversee, supervise, and manage the events of all of your personal angels, and the events that take place where the group of you are concerned, no matter how big, or small. I guess you could say I am your guardian angel supervisor,"

Percival takes a deep breath then continues.

"Now, that's pretty much the whole of it in a nutshell. Do any of you have any questions?"

"Uh, yeah," Joey says, "how did you get into that portal, grab us, and get out so fast?"

Percival glances at Aganon and grins, "tricks of the trade my friend."

"We saw a flash of light and suddenly Joey and Becky were on their back right in front of us. It happened in a matter of a second or two," Eddie exclaims, gesturing at the cleft where the portal was.

"We travel and move differently than ya'll do Eddie, that's as best we can describe it," Aganon says gently.

"You move like that to Aggie?" Robbie asks.

Aganon nods, "when I need to," he says with a smile.

"Wow," Angela says in awe, "pretty cool."

"Yeah," Laura and Becky echo in stereo.

"Ok, so what now?" Eddie says, "Are we still able to travel? What exactly happened?"

"Oh boy," Percival says, trying to get a grasp on how to explain, "this is going to be a bit more difficult to explain."

"They can grasp quite a lot Percy," Aganon says, "give it a try."

"Ok," Percival says getting ready to hand out an explanation as best he can, "here's how it went. There has been a constant battle raging since ya'll, errr you all, *Percival glances at Aganon and rolls his eye and, Aganon grins,* started out on your journey. There is always a battle raging, but it really stepped up once you all accepted your charge. We have been holding the dark forces back quite well. Today, they must have sent in a special attack or a suicide play. They were able to get to Ag and throw him off balance. They attempted to knock him into the portal and leave the rest of you stranded, but we cut the attacker down before he could get a good line on him. Aganon does not see the battle raging while he is in your presence. In fact, I cannot see it now either. I'll have to get back soon. Aganon was too strong for the infiltrator and he merely stumbled. The dark forces can be strong at times. You all provided the strength Ag needed to hold his footing as well as he did. Your prayers are his strength; all of our strength. The attacker never had a chance to see if his attempt succeeded. It never got its feet on the ground."

Percival pauses to check for confusion, "your travel can continue as planned."

"Thanks Percy," Joey says, "can we call you Percy?"

Percival laughs, "Sure you can my friends, and I would be honored."

Joey sticks his hand out to Percival. Percival shakes his hand with a wide grin. Becky steps up to him. He puts his hand out to her; she pushes it aside and hugs him tightly. His grin widens. Eddie and the others shake hands with Percival and thank him for being there to help them.

"Happy trails pardners," Percival says and he bows his head slightly.

They wave, Aganon tips his hat.

"Better watch your step up their Aggie," Percival says with a snicker as he thumbs a gesture toward their portal rock.

Aganon looks up at the rock and his charge turns to look as well.

"You bet I will Percy," Aganon replies and turns back toward him.

"I'll make sure my footing is... what..," Aganon stops. "Bah, he's always doing that."

"What?" Eddie says turning to Percival, but Percival is gone. They all look toward where Percival was standing. He is not there.

"That's how he does things," Aganon says, "Flashes in to lend a hand, then gone in the blink of an eye the next moment. I'm glad ya'll were able to meet him. Give you a better understanding of some of things."

"That was pretty wild Aggie," Laura says, still looking at where Percival used to be.

"He seems like a really nice guy," Angela adds.

"He sure does," Joey adds, "he saved our lives, didn't he Ag."

"In a way, I suppose he did," Aganon says, "but in truth, you were not in much danger as long as you were to stay right where you came in, I would have been able to bring you back, but Percy was lightning fast about it. I think he saw it coming."

"Yeah," Becky says, "he must have."

They all stand in silence for a few minutes to gather their thoughts and courage and focus on the task at hand once again.

"Ok, we have a mission to get back to," Eddie finally says.

"Indeed," Aganon agrees, "shall we."

"Yes, lets." Joey replies. "Let's try this again." He says as he walks up to the rock cleft and waits for Aganon to summon the portal once more.

"You sure you're up for this Joey?" Eddie asks. "You want one of us to go first this time?"

"Nah, I'm still ready to get on with it," Joey replies.

Eddie nods, "you got it brother."

Aganon steps back to the rock formation on the same spot he stood when he was pushed off. He firmly plants his feet once more as his charge gather below for another quick work of prayer. Joey bows his head and follows along, still waiting for his chance to brave his way into the portal a second time.

Aganon draws his lariat, twirls it over his head allowing a large loop to form again. He lets fly with the loop and once again, easily ropes the rock outcropping and pulls the rope tight with the flick of his wrist. He holds the rope and looks down at the portal swirling into existence once more. The scene of the garden of the palace appears again. It is exactly the same, as if they pushed a rewind button on a large movie projector.

Aganon looks at Joey and says, "Ready when you are Joey."

Joey nods and walks through. Becky follows closely behind him, then Eddie, Angela, Laura, and then Robbie. Once Robbie is all the way in Aganon jumps down off the rock into the portal and flips the rope up and off the rock as he goes. The portal winks out almost instantly and leaves a swirling fog of mist in its place. The dust settles and the silence falls on their camp like a shadow.

Chapter 11

After the hail

Aganon and his charge stand in the lush gardens of Pharaohs palace. They are looking upward at the balcony where Pharaoh and Moses are having a heated discussion over the future of the slaves of Egypt; God's people.

Moses again reminds Pharaoh, "Thus sayeth The Lord, 'Let My people go, that they may serve Me, for at this time I will send My plagues to your very heart, and on your servants and on your people, that you may know that there is none like Me in all the earth.'"

Eddie and his friends continue to listen as Moses explains to Pharaoh that his hardened heart will once again cause great devastation on all the land of Egypt. If he does not call in all of the people of Egypt and the livestock, they will all surely die in the coming plague of hail. Moses explains there will be fire in the hail and the sight of it will be unlike anything that has ever been seen in the land of Egypt from its beginning until now.

"Hard to imagine fire mingled with ice. This will really be a sight to see," Joey says in a whisper.

"Indeed it will, Joey," Aganon agrees.

They continue to listen as Pharaoh once again sends Moses and Aaron away in disgust.

"So that's it then. Now the hail comes?" Angela asks quietly.

"Tomorrow at this same time Angela," Eddie answers.

"That's right, I remember now," She replies. "Not a cloud in the sky and no storm on the horizon, and then hail, lightning and fire begin to fall out of a clear blue, mid-day sky."

"Uh huh, what do we do until then?" Robbie asks.

"We wait I guess," Eddie adds.

"Not necessarily. Everybody gatherer in a circle around me, join hands and help me to gather my strength. I'll bring us quickly to the time of the storm," Aganon says.

They gather around Aganon and with hands tightly clasped they pray for the strength of Sampson, the Wisdom of Solomon and the spirit of Elijah. They pray fervently; they pray silently to themselves and for each other.

Aganon draws his lariat and raising a loop in his hand above his head, he begins to twirl it over their heads. As the loop begins to grow larger he bends his wrist and lets the loop drop free of his hand so that he is holding the ropes length. The loop spins and drops down, circling him and his charge. He spins it faster as it begins to lower down over the circle of prayer. As the swirling loop reaches the midriff of his charge it pauses and twirls there in fast tight rotation. Suddenly a light blue halo begins to swirl along the inside edge of the lariat loop and surrounds them.

For a long moment nothing happens but the spin of the rope and the prayer of Eddie and his friends, and then the clouds in the sky begin to slide past more quickly. The stars begin to wink quickly into the darkening night sky, faint at first then growing in brightness. Then suddenly it is dark night and the sky is filled with stars. They waver and dance in the slight rotation of the night sky. Then the stars begin to fade as light begins to dawn in the eastern sky. Aganon continues to twirl his lariat and his charge continues their fervent prayers.

The sky continues to lighten as the stars one at a time wink out for the day sky. Suddenly it's mid morning and the sky shines brightly. The loop continues to twirl as the day flashes by around them. Then, as one fluid motion, Aganon begins to raise the twirling loop back up and over his head. As the twirling rope passes his head he tosses it upward into the air and with lightning speed he coils it back up as it comes down. He puts it back under his coat. A moment later the silent prayers of his charge come to a close and they begin to look up from their reverent time spent with their Maker.

"Did anything change Aggie?" Rebecca asks.

"The day has passed to the next Becky," Aganon replies.

Eddie looks around and notices only the slight difference in the moons position in the late day sky.

"Wow! Look at the moon. It's farther down in the sky. A full day has passed. That's amazing Aggie!" He says in excitement.

"How did you do that Aggie?" Laura gasps in awe.

"The power of God and your prayers, my friends, He is The Almighty," Aganon says in triumph.

"How close is it Ag?" Robbie asks in a soft voice.

"Within moments, not to worry my friends, none of the hail or fire will get to us. We are only observing, not participating," Aganon reassures them.

They nod in understanding and begin to look up at the bright day sky. They see Pharaoh approach on his balcony once again. He also looks up at the bright day sky. He continues to look skyward, then, as if his thoughts summoned the event, hail begins to fall upon his balcony. At first it is soft and light but as it gains in weight it also gains in strength. Soon his entire balcony is white with hail and large stones are beginning to pile up. He ducks in under the doorway and the hail covering the floor begins to waver with fire right before his very eyes. Fire also begins to fall out of the sky in small balls. Some of the fireballs are as large as his head. He notices his city as it begins to crumple under the weight of the storm.

Fires break out all over causing people to run and scream. In the distance crops are flattening and burning at the same time. He looks up again at the sky and there is not a cloud in sight but there is lightning that begins to flash out over the sky. It strikes several locations in the city as it stretches its brilliant light across the hail storm. He lowers his head in shame as his city collapses before his very eyes. There is nothing he can do now but watch.

"I can hear them screaming," Angela whimpers, "All those innocent people caught prisoner by Pharaohs arrogance. It's so sad."

"Millions in history have died to such sad stubbornness; pride and hatred," Aganon adds, "It is not Gods design, but the sinful nature of man himself. Man is so easily led astray by the forces of darkness."

"The fires are burning all over the city," Eddie says, "even the crops outside the city are burning."

"Total destruction," Robbie sighs.
"Many people heard the warning of Moses to Pharaoh and have taken heed. There are God fearing Egyptians in this city that gathered their livestock and families into their homes to save themselves," Aganon says. "I'm sure many have been spared."

"We have to walk through all of this to get out of the city don't we Ag," Angela asks in humble reverence.

"Yes Angela," Aganon answers, "It is the only way out for us. We can wait until the storm is over to go back if you all prefer."

"Yes," Eddie quickly replies, "let's wait awhile."

"It will be over soon," Aganon replies.

They wait and wander around the garden. None of them get very far from the other. The hail falls all around them, and the fires lick at the walls and the lush foliage of the garden. None of it touches them.

They notice that they don't even feel the chill or the heat. It is as if they are separated by an invisible barrier. Finally the hail and fire begins to subside and the lightning also stops. The sky appears to be a very brilliant blue and the day could be such a splendid experience except for the wails and screams coming from the city below. It is as if the winds have brought a howling choir of screams. They can barely stand the sound of it. They gather together again in a circle with hands joined and they pray. They pray silently and heartily as the sounds finally being to fade. Only the occasional moan and wail can be heard. The city is now at work cleaning up the devastation and gathering the dead.

Aganon looks at his charge and ponders a moment the impact the next hour will have on their entire lives. They will have to walk through the macabre mess that is the devastation of God's ninth plague on the land of Egypt. The largest concentration of destruction is right there in the city of Raamses. He knows they will take the sight of all the dead pretty hard. He braces himself for the hours to come and steps forward to start the events in motion.

"We have to prepare to leave this place before night falls completely," He says in a quiet and comforting voice.

Eddie looks up at him and draws his strength for what he knows will be a very difficult journey.

Aganon nods at him and they share a moment where they each know what role they must play in the moments to come; they must be stronger than the rest.

"You're right Ag," Eddie says soberly, "we should be going."

"I'm not sure I can do this Eddie," Angela says meekly.
"I think we have to Angela," Robbie says.

"You're right Robbie," Eddie replies, "we do have to do this." He continues, his tone soft, "This is exactly what we knew we would have to get through, and now the time has come and we must be strong, brave, and let the spirit of The Lord lead us."

"You are all very strong, and you have courageously brought yourselves this far," Aganon says. "There is still much to do, this is only part of it. I'll be ready when you are." He walks across the scorched ice covered gardens and waits at the archway gates leading out of the palace.

"Now is the time," Eddie says, "ready?"

"I'm ready," Joey says with a trembling voice.

Advocate of Time   Craig Allan

"Me too," Rebecca says.

"Okay, let's do this," Laura says, trying to be strong.

Eddie sets out first across the garden toward Aganon, and the others follow him closely. Angela is the last in the line; she hangs back for a few moments walking slowly and looking at the scorched flowers and plants that used to hold such beauty. She continues to move through the ruined garden as the group starts out through the gate right behind Aganon. They make their way through the palace and exit through the front gates into the city street.

The first thing they see is a group of people gathered around a ruined cart. The cart is broken in several pieces and the one wheel is broken in half. There is a hushed murmur of voices as they pass by the group. Angela looks toward the scene as they pass by, Angela sees a person's arm with the palm facing upward laying under the broken cart. Before she can look away she notices that the person is burned badly. The body is frozen into the layers of hail and ice on the ground. She notices all of this before she gets here eyes turned away. She looks at Eddie who has just looked away from the horrible scene. Their eyes lock for a moment and begin to well up with tears. Eddie looks away. He stares forward as they continue to walk toward the other side of town

where they make their portals to leave the man
made city.

They walk a little further and round a corner. They
find a group of Egyptian officials supervising Hebrew
slaves in the task of gathering the bodies of fallen
citizens from the street. Aganon and his charge hurry
by the group as they peel a burned man from the
step of a house. They notice his clothing still smoking
even though he was frozen into the ice.

They begin to cry softly but continue moving more
quickly through the streets, they keep their heads
down and walk briskly following Aganon up the last
stretch of street toward the hillside on the edge of
town.

Robbie glances to his right as they pass a house that
is burning with nobody attempting to put out the
fire. There is a man leaning against the front of the
house. He is dead, his body is badly beaten, and
blood runs from many wounds all over his face and
head. Embers from the burning house land on his
clothes and they begin to catch fire. Joey notices this
and he starts to walk to the man to put out the
flames. Aganon grasps Joeys arm and turns him back.

Joey's eyes meet Aganon's and he says, "We can't
just let him burn Ag."

"We have to Joey," Aganon says with gentle heart-wrenching kindness, "we cannot interfere in any of what happens here. Not ever."

Eddie gently grasps Joey by the hand and pulls him back into the group, "come on Joey, we can make it."

Joey falls back into the group sobbing heavily and covering his face. They continue their forward push for the edge of town and freedom from the sight of the result of this cities proud and arrogant ruler.

As though he generated the thought Eddie speaks up, "remember guys, this mess was caused by Pharaoh himself. God carried out what Pharaoh called down upon himself, his people and his land. It's important that we not lose sight of that."

They nod. Angela says in gasping sobs, "Some of God's lessons were horrible."

Nobody says anything more. They walk in quick steps and in silence. They pass dozens of fallen Egyptians, some whole families with their pets at their side. Dead in the streets, burned in the fire and frozen in the ice. They pass houses where survivors look outward at the horror of what remains of their city. On their faces they see the answer to the question that only Pharaoh will not ask. How long will our King lead us into the punishment of the God of Israel?

They all know, yet Pharaoh will not bow his pride to the power of God Almighty.

Aganon and his charge come to the end of the street and pass through the archway gate to the hillside outside of town. The smoke and haze from the destruction of the city hovers everywhere. There is no safe or pleasant place left to go. As they come to the tree on the base of the hill they collapse on the ground in sobs and cries. Aganon watches as they grieve for the lives of those lost and for those left alive who must deal with the aftermath of such a time. Aganon sits down and silently waits for his charge to regain their composure so they can prepare to leave this land of death.

After thirty minutes of sobbing and embracing, they gather themselves around Aganon. Eddie steps forward and speaks for the rest of them.

"Take us to the tree Ag," Eddie says with a whimper in his voice, "take us to the place where we all feel closest to our maker. We need Him to help us to understand why this happened. We need Him to help us to understand why we needed to see these things for ourselves. We need Him to help us to understand our purpose in all of this." He pauses to wipe his face then continues, "Please get us out of here Ag."

"As you wish Eddie," he says, "you are all very brave. I am honored to be your companion."

He turns to the portal tree, opening his coat Aganon takes out his whip. He draws it back and sets sail to the branch that stretches out toward the burning city. The end of the whip lands and latches on with a whoosh, he draws his arm downward and steps under the branch. The portal immediately swirls into view. They can barely see the water washing on the shore of Lake Pituit. The tree comes into view and they can see their sign. Comfort and calm begins to wash over them as they see the things that bring them peace and joy in The Lord. Eddie looks at Aganon and he nods. Eddie turns to Angela and gestures with his head to the portal. She steps forward, takes his hand and they go through together. Robbie steps up with Rebecca and they join hands and pass through in silence. Last Joey steps up next to Aganon; Laura is behind him with her head down. Joey steps aside and waits as Laura walks up to Aganon. She stands toe to toe with him and looks up into his kind and caring eyes. She looks at him for a long moment then she suddenly embraces him in a tight and loving hug. She holds him for a few moments then finally let's go. She turns to Joey, reaches out for his hand and he offers it. They walk to the portal look at the scene of a memory of home, and they pass through. Aganon is left by himself for a moment. He looks toward Heaven and says,

"Dear Lord Almighty on High, give them strength and understanding. Help me to bring them through this and into the next group of events." He looks lovingly toward home a moment longer. Then he steps through the portal and with a flick and flash of his wrist, he draws the whip back from the tree branch and it trails through behind him. The portal swirls and pulses for a moment then spins in on itself and winks out of existence. The air stirs gently where the portal was and swirls a pocket of smoke, then the air is calm. In the distance, moans and cries can be heard on the air. The sun is setting on the ruins of the Egyptian city of Raamses. The Pharaoh is left with the thought that the Hebrew God will destroy all he has gained in his life. He has to do something.

Aganon and his charge sit silently and reverently as they pray and reflect on the things they had seen. They gather their strength and courage and begin to feel better. The events they have seen have blended in their minds with what they have read over the years in the book of Exodus. Soon, they will be ready to return to the land of Goshen to their hillside where they will plan their next group of events.

Eddie gathers the others together and they talk and pray in a tight circle at the base of their tree. Aganon looks at the sign they posted years ago and agrees that it says true.

Gods place

This is where they come to grow in their walk with Jesus. What a strength these prayer warriors have in Christ. Aganon ponders the things he has learned from them and the thought makes him smile. Eddie gets up and steps over to Aganon.

"What's funny Ag?" He asks.

"Oh, nothing Eddie," he stammers, "I was just thinking of all that I have learned from the group of you."

"You?!" Eddie questions emphatically, "you have learned from us?!"

"Sure Eddie," Aganon replies in earnest, "no one is ever beyond learning something good or new."

"You and your friends have taught me much in these few days we have been together," Aganon assures him, "don't underestimate the gift you have. The gift you all have."

Eddie nods in agreement. "Okay, I think we are all in agreement that we are ready to go back and finish this mission; to draw nearer to God's great work."

"Very well," Aganon says as he turns to the tree and pulls his whip from his coat. Turns to Eddie and asks, "Where to?"

"The last plague Ag," Eddie says with hesitation, "we need to finish this."

Aganon nods somberly and draws back with his whip and snags the reaching arm of the tree they are standing around. The air swirls some leaves in the doorway created. The portal begins to swirl and open in the center as the scene of a darkness appears. Aganon looks again at Eddie,

"The last day of darkness on the land of Egypt before the firstborn of the land are taken," Aganon says, "is everyone ready then?" He asks to the group.

They nod as if one person.

Aganon gestures to the portal of darkness. Eddie steps through followed by Angela, Laura, Robbie, Joey, and then Becky. Aganon follows them in, his whip trailing behind. The portal darkens a bit more then spins out away from its center. It fades away and the tree and the lake are left with the warmth of the day.

Chapter 12

Last plague and the exodus

The sun is setting in the city of Raamses on the night of the worst plague to fall on the land of Egypt in all of history. There is a dark reddish haze in the sky that is making the streets appear to run with blood. In the neighboring land of Goshen the Israelites are free from fear, for the curse is fallen on Egypt.

"The sky has not seen light in three days," Eddie says in a whisper. "Not a single person in Egypt has left their homes. The darkness is so thick that it can even be felt."

"Spoken right from the scriptures Eddie," Aganon replies in a quiet voice.

"It was hard to understand how it was written, but being here and feeling it... I can feel the darkness," Eddie replies.

They stand in silence, huddled in a tight group around Aganon, and they watch. The minutes pass slowly. Nobody speaks or moves, they barely breathe. The darkness surrounds them tightly but it does not penetrate them or their group. They are observers of the events but are not participants. The darkness is still sobering and takes their breath away. Laura raises her hand to see it and has to raise it to within inches of her face before she can finally make out its shape and detail.

"It's like the dark is a fog," She says timidly.

"I think it actually is Laura," Eddie replies.

They look at each other for a moment then back out toward the city they cannot see.

"How long will it last Ag?" Laura asks quietly.

"We have come at exactly the moment that Moses is meeting with Pharaoh over the darkness that has fallen on their land," Aganon replies. "The Egyptians worship many false gods, but the one god they favor above all other is their sun god. These three days of darkness has awakened a fear in them that they have never known. They are beginning to believe that Moses speaks the truth. They are beginning to believe that God Himself is the one and true God and that their destruction will be complete if they do not do as He says and let His children go."

"But Pharaohs heart is still hardened Ag," Robbie adds, "he is not going to let them go yet."

"Yes Robbie," Aganon replies, "you say true. But Pharaoh, as he has done many times before, will tell Moses that he will let them go if he will ask his God to call off the plagues."

"Then as soon as things in his kingdom are restored, he goes back on his word and refuses to free the children of God," Laura adds.

"Yes," Aganon agrees, "and don't forget that The Lord knows Pharaohs heart and his mind. He knows that he will not truly follow God's commandments or His word. God is using the hardness of Pharaohs heart to bring to the Israelites His true purpose. God will make an example of Egypt and all who worship false gods and ignore the word and law of God Almighty."

"Yeah," Joey adds, "Pharaoh worships himself as god and elevates himself over his people as their god. How can anyone live like that for very long before the one true God shows them the truth about his mighty reign?"

"Pharaoh will fall soon enough," Eddie continues their dialogue, "it is written that God hardens Pharaohs heart so that he will follow his own actions directly into Gods plan. God will be glorified and

Pharaoh will be the one who is the example for the entire world to see."

"Are we going to see Moses speak with Pharaoh in regard to the last plague?" Robbie asks to everyone.

Aganon looks at them questioningly, turns and walks up to the rock outcropping and awaits their decision. Eddie and Angela sit closely together near the fire; the others are huddled a few feet from them in a small group as they pray together. Angela is deep in prayer. Eddie looks around at everyone, and then he looks up at Aganon perched on his rock. He says a short prayer in preparation of their next journey.

"Dear, Lord God, please help us to see with open eyes the things You have meant for us to see. Help us to know Your will in all of this. We are Your servants and Lord God, we wish only that you would use us and teach us. Help us to have steadfast hearts and the strength that only You can provide. We thank You and praise You for this rare and wonderful opportunity to take part in Your miracle of deliverance and grace. You are an awesome God. Thank you for choosing me. In Jesus name we pray. Amen." He finishes his prayer and continues to meditate with his head bowed.

Angela reaches over and touches his shoulder and he reaches up and put his hand on hers. They continue to be in God's presence for a moment longer. They look up at each other and smile warmly. Angela looks over at the others still with their heads bowed in reverence.

"Eddie," she says quietly, "we have seen things no other person in our lives have even considered or conceived of," she pauses, "how we will be able to bear it all?"

"This is God's plan Angela," Eddie warmly replies, "He is on His throne; He knows what we can, and cannot bear. He knows about all of it."

"Yes, I know that," She replies shortly. "But this will all be an experience we have never even come close to considering. Reading of it, yes, but we are seeing it all first hand. Aren't you concerned about how it will affect you in the future?

Eddie thinks about her question," I know God will give us the strength we need Angela. If we are faithful, He will be faithful too."

She considers her own faith then nods. They sit in silence for a little while. The others begin to come over. They stand up and gather together. When they have all gathered they have a group prayer. The prayer is short and powerful. Once they have all spoken to God the things they feel they turn to face Aganon and their next portal.

"We wish to see Moses tell Pharaoh he has condemned his own people to death," Eddie says to Aganon as if he is reading the thoughts of his group of friends. The others nod in agreement.

"Moses speaks to Pharaoh this very moment. We will travel to the moment where Moses makes his demand for God," Aganon says. "Are ya'll ready?"

"Yep, I reckon we are," Eddie replies with a grin.

Aganon nods and draws his lariat. He twirls it over his head creating a large loop as it passes over him. He tosses it deftly to the rock and snags it easily with fluid motion. He draws the lariats rope tight with a sharp tug. The portal beneath the rope begins to appear. They watch as the portal swims and swirls into existence. It appears as a dance of lights swirling from a central point of light. The gateway swells, spins and develops into a scene with two men standing many feet apart in an obvious disagreement. They know immediately that it is Pharaoh and Moses. Aaron is standing next to Moses. He is holding the staff that God has used so many times to demonstrate his power.

"Where are they Ag?" Becky asks.

"Looks like they are in the courtyard garden outside of Pharaohs throne-room," Aganon replies.

"That's a good location for us to stand back and still see what's going on," Eddie says.

"Let's do this," Robbie says, and steps up to the portal. He looks up at Aganon holding the rope and looking firm and steady.

"God's speed Ag," and he steps through.

Becky follows right behind him without hesitation. The others follow right behind her. After they are all in and Aganon can see them lining up, he drops into the portal and flicks the rope up and off the rock as he falls through. The portal shows the seven of them standing in the garden with Pharaoh and Moses in the background. The last thing the portal shows is Aganon drawing up his lariat and stowing it under his coat. The portal shudders and flickers. Then it flashes out instantly. A puff of dust rises up from the cleft in the rocks where the portal was, then the dust settles and the surrounding area is silent and calm.

Aganon and his charge stand in silence listening as Pharaoh speaks, "Go, serve the Lord; only let your flocks and your herds be kept back. Let your little ones also go with you."

Moses replies, "You must also give us sacrifices and burnt offerings, that we may sacrifice to the Lord our God. Our livestock shall go with us; not a hoof shall be left behind."

And once again Pharaoh's heart was hardened to the bidding of Moses by command of God on High.

"Get away from me! Take heed to yourself and see my face no more! For in the day you see my face you shall die!"

"There it is," Joey sighs, "the death decree that Pharaoh uttered to the whole of the land of Egypt."

"You have spoken well," Moses says, "I will never see your face again." Moses continues to speak, "Thus says the Lord: 'About midnight I will go out into the midst of Egypt; and all the firstborn in the land of Egypt shall die; from the firstborn of Pharaoh who sits on his throne, even to the firstborn of the female servant who is behind the hand mill, and all the firstborn of the animals. Then there shall be a great cry throughout all the land of Egypt, such as was not like it before, nor shall be like it again. But against none of the children of Israel shall a dog move its tongue, against man or beast that you may know that the Lord does make a difference between the Egyptians and Israel.'" Moses pauses in a dead stare at Pharaoh. Pharaoh's face is drawn tight in defiant anger, but he is unable to speak or raise his hand to him. Moses continues, "And all these, your servants shall come down to me and bow down to me, saying 'Get out, and all that people who follow you!' After that I will go out."

Moses turns and storms out of the garden with righteous anger. Aaron follows behind him.

Pharaoh is left in a fuming anger over the conversation that has taken place. No person living or dead has ever been permitted to speak to a god-like Pharaoh, and here this prophet of the God of Israel makes demands and threats. Pharaoh storms out of the garden into his throne-room and they can hear his shouts of anger all the way from his inner chambers.

"He's furious," Angela whispers.

"Yeah," Robbie adds, "Moses just told him how it is. I don't think he is used to that."

"I think that it's important for us to remember that every single one of these plagues and curses are the work of Pharaoh himself," Eddie says, "he had a chance before the devastation of every one of these events to repent and turn from his wicked ways. He chose not to every single time. He is arrogant, pompous, ungodly, and evil. He has brought down the wrath of God upon himself, his people and his lands. Let's try to remember that in the days to come."

"It has begun my friends," Aganon tells them somberly, "I think it best if we start to make our way out of the city."

"Is it time?" Eddie asks in a short and pointed question.

"Yes," Aganon replies, "midnight is the time set by God himself for the death of all the firstborn of Egypt. We should get going. It's dark and it will take us awhile to get out of the city." "Yeah," Laura adds, "let's get out of here."

They file out of the gardens toward the great halls that lead out of the palace to the inner city, then to the darkened streets. Their dim journey will be long and they will have to battle their fear. God is with them, the victory is already theirs.

Aganon and his charge make their hillside refuge only twenty minutes before the fall of midnight. They gather themselves at the base of the tree outside of the city walls. They feel the tension and the fear building within them. Each of them entertains their own thoughts of the hours to come when the final plague falls on the land of Egypt. They each think that it might be better to summon a portal and flee from this certain death. But they stand fast and await the events to come. They have the same faithful promise as the children of Israel.

The one promise that each of them loses sight of in the stiffening fear is that their price has already been paid. They each have a promise that not a single member of the Hebrews has; that promise is the gift of eternal life through Christ Jesus. The price Jesus paid for them was paid many centuries after the flight of the Israelites from the land of Egypt. Even though this life changing promise exists for each of them, they still feel the fear and ominous approach of the night of death. No event like it has ever happened in the history of Egypt and no other event will ever come close. This is the night that Pharaoh uttered a death sentence for his own son and all the first born children of his entire nation, just as Pharaoh before him did for the newborn boys of the Hebrews forty years ago.

Aganon and his charge kneel silently outside the city walls of Raamses as the hour of midnight falls on the land of Egypt.

As promised, the Lord God almighty descends his presence in a white mist of cloud and light from the heavens above. Aganon and his charge do not look upon the presence of God as he descends but they keep their heads lowered in reverence and prayer. The fine mist descends to the ground and covers the entire land of Egypt. Not a single wisp or glimmer of Gods Holy presence reaches outside the borders of Egypt to any other lands. It touches and reaches only to the farthest and deepest parts of all of Pharaohs land. The luminescent presence of God settles and stills on the ground. His presence wavers and flows as though it were fluid. Throughout all the lands, even those reaching outside of Egypt, a reverent hush of complete silence falls.

The stillness stretches out for several minutes as the faithful of God pray and the faithless hold their breath.

Then, as if a siphon was started from high within the heavens, Gods presence begins to swirl upward very slowly from the center of the palace of Thutmose, the Pharaoh of Egypt. Within the swirl of mist that is the very presence of God, a faint shimmering light can be seen spiraling into the center of the column that is ascending to the heavens. As the vortex of God's presence begins to swirl faster pulling the mist of his glorious visitation out of the streets of Raamses and the land of Egypt, shimmering lights are being drawn into the flow and are drifting up with the whirling funnel, rising into the sky. More and more lights begin to flood into the funnel as it spins faster and stretch higher. The funnel is filled with lights, spinning and swirling.

Advocate of Time   Craig Allan

Then as suddenly as God made his way into the land of Egypt, He is gone into the heavens and with him the life force of the first born of every Egyptian person, animal, fish, reptile and living thing within Egypt's borders. Within moments of the close of the heavens and the withdrawal of the presence of Almighty God, a steady and gut wrenching wail rises from the land. The noise begins in a low and echoing moan and rises within moments to a siren of high pitched shrieks, wails, screams, and shouts. The sound is deafening and Aganon and his charge bury their heads in their hands and try to hide from its piercing sound.

The noise continues for a full thirty minutes at a fevered pitch, and then it begins to fade to a steady mournful song as if sung by a choir of thousands of voices, millions of voices. And that is exactly what it is, hundreds of thousands, even millions of voices all crying out in pain and suffering for the loss of their loved ones; the sound of all living things mourning their grievous loss.

On the very peak of this sorrowful song is Pharaoh and his queen, crying and mourning for the loss of their only son; the heir to the throne of Egypt.

As the mourns and cries continue through the night Aganon raises his whip and snaps the limb they use to make their way through portals. The portal they create is to the land of the Red Sea. As each of them pass through the portal a peace fills their ears as calm and silent bliss washes over them on the other side. Eddie and Angela walk in last, right on their heels Aganon strides through pulling his whip behind him. Then, as if even the portal cannot stand the sound of the cries of death on the wind any longer, it winks out instantly leaving no scene of the travelers no wind or dust. It is gone and the night is left with its sobs and screams of death and destruction.

Chapter 13

Before the water

Eddie and Angela are the last through the portal. Aganon follows behind them closely. They breathe a sigh of relief as they plop down on the ground in the warm sun and quiet breeze. Aganon sets out to gather wood for a fire and gives them time to rest and take refreshment before they decide what to do next.

"That was pretty intense," Joey says with tears in his eyes.

"Uh huh," Becky agrees.

"I have never heard anything like that in all my life," Eddie says in astonishment.

"I have," Laura offers in quiet reverence, "I was at the scene of an earthquake in California a few years ago where a series of buildings collapsed and trapped over a thousand people within a city block. They setup a triage in the parking lot across the street where I helped as much as I could. The sound of people grieving their lost loved ones and the cries of injured people mixed together was awful. I thought I would never forget that sound as long as I lived, until now," She drops her face into her hands and sobs.

Eddie gets up and walks over to where she is sitting. He sits down next to Laura and gently takes her into his arms. She sobs loudly while he holds her and softly tells her to go ahead and let it out. Robbie gets up and comforts her as well. He kneels next to her and puts his hands on her shoulders and silently prays. The others get up and gather around their friends and pray. They pray for peace, for love, for understanding and joy. They pray for the strength to go on, and to face the things they must see. They pray for each other and they pray for those left in ruins in Egypt. Mostly, they pray for the children of Israel as they start their long journey to the land of freedom.

They fall silent after awhile and wait for Laura to regain her composure. She finally lifts her head and hugs Eddie. One at a time the others hug her and go back to sitting in a circle around the fire Aganon has made for them.

Eddie and Laura walk to the fire and sit down. They stare at the warm and joyous flames for awhile as they consider the things they have seen.

"Did anyone see what was happening back there?" Robbie asks.

"I glanced up a couple of times to get an idea of what exactly was going on," Eddie admits, "it was not at all like I had thought it would be."

"Yeah," Angela says, "I had a couple looks myself."

"The movies and the imagination, even the way it is written in Exodus make it sound as if The Lord himself would be walking through all of Egypt killing things. But that's not how it was at all."

"He is a God of love. It makes perfect sense the way it happened," Eddie adds, "even though it was a curse the Pharaoh himself brought upon his land, even then God was as kind and gentle as He has always been."

"God is so good," Becky adds.

"Amen Becky," Joey agrees, "Amen."

"Yeah," Angela interjects, "He is so amazing in His kindness and love for all mankind. We sure don't deserve it."

"You do more than others I'd say," Aganon chimes in, "but it is written that all have sinned and fallen short of the glory of God."

"Romans 3:23," Eddie confirms.

"Was that the real presence of God Ag?" Laura innocently asks.

"God has many forms and shapes," Aganon says, "He can take on any shape and form he wishes, we never actually see his form, He is pure light, power, spirit, glory and life."

"This time he was in the midst of a mist or a fog," Eddie adds.

"Yeah," Angela says, "it was beautiful and terrible at the same time."

"God can be all of those things," Aganon says, "just remember who is called of Him, who He loves and who has provoked His anger by their stubborn and foolish acts."

They nod and take some time to ponder the things they have spoken of and what they have seen. Aganon sets their pack in front of him and opens it. He looks at its contents for a moment then passes the pack to Eddie who takes out what he wants and passes it on. They eat, visit, reflect and rest for a full two hours before they discuss any further adventures or travel. Eddie knows that the very next place and ultimately the last place they will go will be to the Red Sea crossing at the Gulf of Aqaba. For now they will take some time to gather their strength. In this place, there is all the time in the world for them. They are in no hurry.

Eddie stands on the hillside of Migdol looking outward toward the Gulf of Aqaba. The mountains surrounding the gulf create an ominous feeling of contrast between the blue water and black rock hills that border it. The cleft in the rock formations will allow for the stream of Hebrew travelers to funnel into the large beached area along the western shore of the gulf. In the distance he can see Baal-Zephon across the water and farther to the south and east is Mt. Sinai, where they will find their instructions for their future. Eddie remembers what Jesus said in the gospel of John of these six hundred thousand men with their women and children numbering probably around three million. He spoke deliberately that of all of those freed from the slavery of Egypt, the adult population will only see two or three that will enter into salvation at Christ's Second Advent. Eddie wonders at that huge number of people. So many will perish by their own stubborn and disobedient mistakes, so many will simply defiantly resist Moses' law brought down from God himself, and will be slain by the hand of their own family.

"Dear God, why is man, whom you made in your image, so stubborn and hard hearted? Why did You go through so much trouble to free them just so that they would perish? I don't understand the folly of man, whom I share the same fate and destiny." He hangs his head in shame and humility. He is so caught up in the moment of sadness that he does not hear Angela come up behind him.

 She stands there for awhile listening to him pray, then stepping up next to him, she leans her head on his shoulder and looks off into the darkening sky of the east. They stand in silence for the longest time before she finally speaks, "Eddie," she says, "why do you suppose all those people just kept on doing what God had so clearly instructed them against?"

"Stubbornness I suppose," he replies.

"I just don't understand it," She says, "God's gift is so free, and the life of His service is not such a hard task. So much to throw away, when one just simply has to trust and obey."

"I know," he says sadly, "it makes no sense to us, but these people were slaves in an Egyptian land for who knows how long. They probably had a hard time changing their ways."

"They had over forty years," she replies shortly, "seems to me; that that's easily enough time to change your ways, several generations worth."

"True enough Angela," Eddie says in a simple reply.

"It makes me sad and angry at the same time," She says sharply.

"I know," he says putting his arm around her, "me too."

They stand there awhile longer as the night sky begins to make its way across the eastern sky. They watch the first, brightest stars come out. They remind them of the simple things in life and how God does listen and does answer prayers.

"We better get back," Eddie says after a long silence.

"Yeah," she says.

They turn and walk back to the fire arm in arm. They find the innocence and simplicity of their strong bond of friendship comforting. They arrive at the fire and sit down and listen in on the conversation going on with the others.

"The view is amazing," Laura says to Eddie and Angela

"Yeah," Eddie answers, "the blue water contrasted against the black mountains is something of a sight. It's going to be a beautiful and amazing thing to see God work his miracle with all of it."

"I'm looking forward to it," Robbie chimes in, "have been for this whole trip."

"I think this one will make the whole thing come together in one great act of God," Angela adds, "will make it all worthwhile."

"Yeah," Laura adds, "I think so too."

"So what's next Ag?" Laura asks playfully.

"Well," Aganon replies, "so far we are in the right spot to see the entire march of the freed nation of Israel funnel right through that canyon down there. It's called Wadi Watir. I'm guessing they will be coming through first thing in the morning. They have been walking day and night for six days."

"So the true and biblical location of Pi-hahiroth is right there at the beach. Where the Wadi Watir empties to the open area of Migdol along the Gulf of Aqaba," Eddie suggests.

"You say true Eddie," Aganon answers.

"But in our bible maps and in historical books, Pi-Hariroth is said to be the marsh of reeds north of the Gulf of Suez," Angela adds. "For centuries there has been a debate over the true location of the Red Sea crossing."

"And we are going to see the fact of the event first hand right here," Robbie says in astonishment, "sweet!"

"That's why we are here," Aganon replies, "This is the best vantage point in all of Migdol for a view of the crossing. Notice the rocky hills surrounding the beached area below. Pharaoh will watch from afar and think that the Israelites are trapped by the land and that they are confused and lost. That is when he will send his army to attack them and they will flee across the water right down there." He points to an underwater land bridge that seems to have been set in place for this very event.

"It looks as though this location was handpicked by God himself for this very purpose," Laura says.

"It sure does," Eddie adds. "Like He has been planning this set of events all along."

"What an awesome God we serve," Robbie says dreamily while looking out over the water.

"You know," Eddie says thoughtfully, "our bible maps show a completely different route of the exodus than is written right there in the book of Exodus. In chapter fourteen God even tells Moses to turn and camp before Pi-hahiroth between Migdol and the sea. The maps in our bibles show in several places that the crossing took place at the northern part of the Gulf of Suez."

Eddie looks off into the distance to the west, pausing to consider the distance and then continues, "That whole theory is incorrect considering that the bible does say that Moses led the children of Israel out of Egypt before crossing the Red Sea. The location the maps show for the crossing is clearly within the borders of Egypt," Eddie continues.

"Another thing worth considering is that the book of Exodus says they marched day and night for almost a week before Pharaoh and his army caught up with them; six days and nights. How can the historical location be possible if it was such a short distance from Raamses? It's in the region north of the Gulf of Suez, now that I can see the way it actually happened, it all makes perfect sense."

"I never understood the maps in the back of my bible that showed several alternate routes of the crossing." Joey adds, "It's as though nobody was sure where they crossed."

"That's because historians and archeologists have been looking in the wrong places all this time," Eddie paused then said in awe, "Amazing."

"Wow," Angela says, "I never knew that the Red Sea crossing location was in dispute."

"Only in historical circles I think Angela," Eddie replies. "Nobody ever thought to ask where the actual location of Pi-hahiroth and Migdol were."

They fall silent, each considering the miraculous act of God they will witness.

Finally Robbie breaks the long silence, "So that means that the whole theory about where Mt. Sinai is located is wrong as well, doesn't it."

They all take a moment to consider the location on their maps then Eddie nods, then replies "I think so," he says with excitement in his voice, "wasn't there some sort of big political event about twenty years ago surrounding this guy who discovered the actual location of Mt. Sinai in Saudi Arabia?"

"Yeah," Angela says, "this professor type guy, sometime around 1984 or so, what was his name?"

"Ronald Wyatt," Joey answers.

"Yeah," she shoots back, "that's the guy. He was held prisoner by Saudi military because they thought he was spying."

"They eventually let him go," Eddie says, "in exchange for him taking them to the exact location he found."

"Later," he continues, "When Ron and his group tried to go back to investigate the same area, they found the whole placed fenced by the Saudi government.

Guess they didn't want anyone snooping around there anymore."

"Yeah," Robbie adds, "I remember hearing about that too."

"It's finally starting to come together," Eddie adds.

Silence falls again as they now look off to the east toward the real location of Mt. Sinai where Moses and approximately three million Hebrews will live and wander for more than forty years.

"Sad what happened to all of them," Laura offers, breaking the silence. They nod in agreement and once again there is silence.

Eddie and his friends gather around the fire and curl up to sleep. Aganon wanders the outskirts of their camp looking for a good location for portal travel. It has been a hectic week and his charge seems to be holding up pretty well. The personal experience has drawn from them the best of their abilities and intellect. Aganon finds an outcropping of rock only forty yards from the fire. It has two columns of stone jutting skyward like a pair of fingers in a 'V' shape.

"This will do nicely," he says to the night.

"Looks good to me too Aggie," Percival answers as he steps out from behind the fingers of stone.

"I figured you were hanging around here somewhere," Aganon replies. "I could feel your gravity."

"I thought so," Percival says, "not going to pull anything past you Aggie ol' buddy."

"Was there much resistance while The Lord descended upon the land the night the firstborn were taken?" Aganon asks somberly.

Percival asks, "Resistance?" "I assume you mean from the dark forces. As for the task The Lord had to complete, no. The darkness could not penetrate his countenance. There was a great deal of attack upon your charge. But not a single attacker got even close. Your charges prayer cover is stronger than any I have ever seen." Percival glance toward the fire then adds, "They have a great faith and love of The Lord."

"That they do my friend," Aganon replies proudly also looking in direction of the fire.

"Tomorrow they will see things that few will be able to share a personal account of in the kingdom of heaven," Percival says somberly.

"They know," Aganon adds, "they have a great knowledge of the scriptures. They are aware of the loss of the entire tribe of Israel in those forty years.

They will share the account with Moses himself, as well as Joshua and a few others."

"They are so strong," Percival reflects.

Aganon nods and takes in the thought. Percival turns back to the rocks Aganon has found for a portal.

"What are your plans for this formation my ol' friend?" Percival asks with a tone of playfulness. "They look a little tall. Are you planning to leap to the top to make your way?"
"I'm not going to give the darkness another shot at me," Aganon replies. "I'll fasten to one finger then simply draw the rope across the other at my height and loop it around for a secure cross tie."

"Yeah," Percival agrees, "sounds good. Well buddy, I gotta be off, was great to talk with you again. Keep up the good work. I think The Most High is quite pleased with the progress so far. God's speed and grace Aggie."

"Thanks Percy, God's grace and speed," Aganon replies proudly and thrusts out his hand to him. Percival takes his hand and they shake like old friends who have come together again after a long time.

"I like the traditions you have adopted Aggie," Percival says with a wide smile, "they are pleasant." With that, Percival turns and walks through the rock fingers and vanishes as though he passed through a portal. Aganon is left standing alone again. "Show off," he says with a huge grin on his face. He starts back toward the fire where he will sit and watch his charge sleeping while they wait for the sun to rise on a new day and a new adventure.

Chapter 14

The Red Sea crossing

Eddie rises with his hair tossed and twisted all around his head as though he just stood in a tornado. Angela sits up a few feet from him. She looks at him and laughs quietly to herself. He hears her but pretends not to notice. They sit there a few minutes while the others rise and look around. Eddie gathers his belongings and packs them up and the others do the same. They get their personal duties finished then gather over near Aganon who is still sitting at the base of a steep hill. He is looking out to the east over the water. The view is spectacular.

"Good morning Aggie," Robbie says in greeting.

"Mornin' Robbie," Aganon replies, "you sleep well?"

"Sure did buddy," Robbie says, "this place is like a sleep factory or something. I think I've never slept better."

"That's for sure," Becky adds, "you snored like a top fuel funny car on race day."

They all burst out laughing including Robbie.

"I bet I did," he says still laughing, "I always forget to roll over to my side when I sleep."

"So what's the game plan today Aggie?" Laura asks.

"Well Laura," Aganon replies, "we are gonna see us a spectacular miracle from The Most High God. But first, we get you all something to eat."

"Works for me," Joey says as he brings up the last of them to gather up around Aganon. Aganon hands Joey the pack. Joey takes what he needs and passes it along to the others. They sit and eat, they visit and talk about all the things that have happened and what they have seen so far. They spend an hour preparing for the day, when it looks as though they are all ready to go Aganon stands up.

"If you are all ready," he says, "I'll join you in a word of prayer, then we'll be off. The portal site is just forty yards up the hill."

"Sounds like a plan," Eddie says standing up. "Who will lead us this morning?"

"I will," Becky says as she stands up.
"Cool," Eddie says. "Shall we gather up and join hands."

They gather in a circle with Aganon and they join hands. They bow their heads and Becky leads them in a earnest and thankful petition. She mentions all they have seen and what has happened. She thanks God for the strength he has given each of them and for the opportunity He has given. She thanks Him for Aganon and his guidance and protection. She thanks Him for Percival and his protection. She asks God to look after them as they witness His divine hand in the events of the day. She finishes up with a few words of praise to Him and then they all say 'Amen'.

"Okay," Aganon says after they have raised their heads and dropped hands. "Let's do this. Follow me."

They file in behind Aganon as he starts up the hill toward the rock fingers. The walk is brisk but short. They gather at the base of the rocks as Aganon steps up to the one on their right and draws out his lariat out of his coat.

"As we stand here right now the nation of Israel has gathered below at the beach of Pi-hahiroth. They have made their way through the Wadi Watir and are trapped at the sea. They are surrounded on all sides by mountains and Pharaohs armies are bearing down on them. We will port in on the beach just south of the crossing site. We'll be right near the water so we must be careful not to go near the water or the Israelites. Not to mention the Egyptians. The slightest interference in what takes place today could cause disastrous results. Remember, we are only observers from afar." He pauses for a moment to reflect, and then continues.

"We will stay in our location for the entire event. When we arrive, it will be moments before Moses addresses God's people to get into the water. The pillar of flame will be at the mouth of the Wadi holding the forces of Pharaoh back while Moses gets them to cross over the dry ground. This will all take place this evening as the sun sets. During the course of the night God will send the east wind to blow hard, parting the sea and drying the ground. The Israelites' will cross and after they are almost out on the other side God will move the pillar of fire away from the mouth of the Wadi and the Egyptians will charge into the sea after them." Aganon looks from to another of them.

"This whole movement of millions of people will take all night. At just about sunrise the next morning Moses will stretch out his staff over the waters as The Lord instructs him. Pharaoh and his armies will be in the midst of the path through the water. They will be fighting with their chariots and be trying to pursue Israel in confusion. At the moment Moses stretches out his staff the east wind will cease. The water that is being held back and frozen by the wind will melt away almost instantly when the sun comes upon it. The Egyptians will see this and try to flee back toward the Wadi, but they will not get there. The waters will consume them and they will perish. For it is written." Aganon takes a moment to consider the faces of his charge, and then he continues.

"There will be thousands of dead washing up on the beaches for days. It will be a ghastly site. Pharaoh will be lost in the waters as well. There will be some Egyptians that will have made it out. They will return to tell the story of how The Lord fought for Israel. We will depart the beach back the way of the Wadi and will make our portal away from here within the canyon walls, so, any questions?"

There is a long silence then Eddie speaks up. "I think we have a pretty good grasp on what will happen, I think we are ready."

Aganon looks at the faces of all of them and nods. He turns to the rocks and whirls his lariat in the air over his head. He easily sends the loop sailing and ropes the left rock. He pulls back sharply closing the loop quickly. He steps to the rock on the right and tosses up some slack from his rope to the tip of the rock and fastens a hitch around it. The rope crosses the fingers of rock about seven feet up and closes the gap, creating another doorway. Instantly a puff of dust is kicked up from the ground as color begins to swirl in the center of the doorway. In the center of the swirl of color an eye appears and a scene of the front of the crowd of the nation of Israel comes into view.

The scene grows wider and taller gradually as the portal grows in size. Moses is seen standing on a tall group of rocks near the water's edge. They can see the sky darkening in the east and part of it glowing in the west as the sun sets. They can tell they are looking north from the south of the entire mass of the Hebrew slaves freed from Egypt. The portal comes completely into view and the swirling only continues faintly at the outer edges. Aganon looks to his charge.

"Are we ready for this?" He asks.

"Ready as we'll ever be I guess," Robbie says courageously and he steps up to the portal.

"Who's coming with me?" He says with his hand reached out behind him.

"Me," Laura says immediately, "wait for me," she says as she steps up takes his hand and walks into the portal with Robbie in tow.

"Well," Eddie says, "no better time than the present. Angela?" He says reaching his hand out to her. She step up, takes his hand and they walk through the portal together.

Joey looks at Becky and she smiles gently.

"Ready?" He asks her with his hand out to her.

"Yep," she answers taking his hand as she steps up to the portal. They also walk through together.

"They never cease to amaze me Lord," Aganon says looking skyward. He steps into the portal and in an amazing display of a dance of rope, he flicks his wrist and the slack of the rope spins skyward. It unwraps from the right rock and spins off the left, loosening the lariat loop. It twists and spins skyward briefly then falls as Aganon quickly draws it up while walking through then he joins the others as they watch Moses address the people. The portal begins to swirl backwards and shrink in size as the scene of the Red Sea crossing fades and washes out. The portal continues to shrink in a reverse rotation until it is a small swirling storm of pink with highlights of deep purple. Then as quickly as it appeared, it is gone. The dust stirs where it was born into existence, and then the dust settles and the air is calm as though nothing was ever there.

On the shore of the Gulf of Aqaba the nation of Israel listens and groans as Moses tells them that they need to have a greater faith and trust in their God. Moses raises his arms with the staff of Aaron in his right hand he addresses them one last time before they lose hope and faith completely.

"The Almighty has this day saved you from your oppression and your captivity. Fear not; watch and tremble at the salvation and deliverance of your Great God. Your Great God demands that you step forward in faith and see His great works." Moses turns to the sea and stretches out his hands with Aaron's rod pointing toward the waters.

Some time passes then the bravest of the Hebrews step forward into the waters in faith. Suddenly the wind begins to howl and drive the clouds and the dust from above the beach. The funnels of wind push at the waters and they begin to retreat and billow as if being pushed by Gods hand. The children of Israel watch as the wind pushes and divides the waters of the sea and parts them all the way to the sea floor. The wind billows and gushes with such force and strength that the ocean floor is dried and the people walk as if on dry ground. Moses stands with his arms outstretched toward heaven. Slowly, the bravest of the people begin to step out in faith into the valley created in the sea. As they begin to progress into the seas floor they see the walls of water on the side being forced and frozen in place by the howling freezing winds. They continue to push forward in faith. Slowly, but surely, the entire nation of Israel makes its way into the valley of the Red Sea. As the

Exodus continues the fiery pillar holds back the armies of Pharaoh and confuses their pursuit.

Eddie and the others watch in awe and amazement as the greatest work and miracle they have ever read in the bible unfolds right in front of them. Eddie steps forward two steps and Aganon reaches out to him and grasps his shoulder. Eddie stops, his face awash with delight and amazement.

"I can't believe it Ag." Eddie says in a whisper. "It's happening exactly as we imagined."

"You can't go any closer Eddie," Aganon reminds him.

Eddie stands still and watches in amazement. The water has fallen away into a canyon with vertical walls of ice holding back the sea on both sides. The water that has been displaced has caused the water-line along the beach to raise slightly, the surf washes in and out gently, even up against the frozen walls of the Red Sea crossing. The Israelites continue their flight across the dried sea floor. As they pass their way through the icy, chilly valley of ice, the wind continues its flight through the valley along the ice walls. Amazingly the air is calm along the center of the valley where the Israelites make their passage to freedom and new life. Moses makes his way along with the exodus of his people as soon as their passage begins to flow reliably. An hour passes as they make their way through, then two hours. Eddie and his friends simply watch in amazement as three million or so people cross an eleven mile wide gulf of water and stay completely dry.

"Can we go across with them Ag?" Laura asks in delight.

"It's too risky Laura," Aganon answers apologetically. "I cannot take that risk with your well being my dear friend. I am sorry."

"Can we find a place to make a portal and travel to the other side?" She asks in excitement.

"That we can do," he answers.

"Let's wait to see the Egyptians enter first," Robbie adds.

"Yeah," Eddie says, "Let's wait a bit longer."

They stand and watch as the two knives of wind blow the water into ice, and the entire nation of Israel walk through the Red Sea. Eventually the Israelites make their way halfway through and light begins to dawn in the east.

"The sun is coming up already Ag!" Robbie says in a shout.

"Time has just blasted by," Joey adds.

"Now they will pursue them," Eddie adds.

No sooner does he finish those words then the pillar of fire wanes and flags. It twist sideways a bit then drawn upward, and then winks out. The Egyptians are now free to view the opening in the Red Sea and they can see the last of the Israelites making their way through the sea floor almost five miles away. Pharaoh gives the order to charge in and capture them. So the Egyptian army with its chariots and horsemen, with its soldiers on foot with spears and shields charges into the opening in the Red Sea. Pharaoh leads the way with his scepter drawn and pointing out in front of him. His face is drawn back in a battle cry; he is filled with rage and with fear.

The Egyptians spend an hour following the Israelites when the wind begins to fade. The sun breaks over the eastern horizon and the ice walls begin to melt, sending water trickling into the canyon where the Israelites just passed on dry land. The sand becomes a muddy trap and the chariots lose their grip. The wheels begin to slip and break. The army begins to fall behind. As the water begins to fall and run faster, some of the Egyptians cry out that The Lord fights for the Israelites and they retreat back the way they had come. Most of them continue their pursuit of the Hebrew slaves they have spent so many years kicking into submission. Pharaohs' army is loyal and they continue to follow him, even to their doom.

Eddie turns to Aganon and points back toward the Wadi Watir.

"We can find a place to open a portal to the other side. I don't think I want to see the fleeing army of Pharaoh being crushed by water on this side."

"Yeah," Angela adds, "I think we should head over to the other side." They are almost yelling now as the shouts of the Egyptians that have retreated echo through the melting icy canyon. The cracks and pings of the ice add to the hightened noise. Aganon nods and turns toward the pathway that leads to the canyon through the mountains of Migdol. They make their way quickly into the canyon. Right away Aganon spots a cleft in the rocks very near to the mouth of the Wadi. He leaps up quickly to the top of the cleft as the others gather below and wait for their passage. They quickly bow their heads and say a word of prayer so that they may keep their calm and accept things for the way they will happen, and that God will be glorified in all they see and do.

Aganon stands over the top of the cleft with his legs spread wide, bridging the top of the opening, closing the doorway with his body. A portal begins to swirl into view and then appears instantly. They can all see the scene of the parted Red Sea with ice walls and Israelite families with livestock and wagons making their way up the hill out of the icy canyon. In the distance they can see the glint of light from the shiny armor and shields of the pursuing Egyptian army. Eddie steps up to the portal and steps through without looking around or back. Angela and Laura follow close behind him. Then the others go right behind. Once the last one has gone through Aganon drops off the rocks through the portal. When his feet touch the ground on the other side, the portal winks out and there is nothing.

On the eastern side of the Gulf of Aqaba the flood of Israelites continues as Moses stands above the flow with his eyes turned toward heaven. The last of the nation of Israel file out of the canyon and they fall back behind Moses. Moses looks directly at Pharaoh in his fruitless pursuit of him and Gods people through the valley of mud and myrrh that has been created by the melting ice and running sea water coming through the cracks in the ice.

Pharaoh looks upward toward Moses standing on the rocks less than a half a mile away. His pursuit has been nearly halted completely as his chariot sinks in the sinking sands of the sea floor. Moses and Pharaoh lock eyes and stare at each other for a full minute. Then Moses raises his arms to heaven with Aaron's staff outstretched again in his right hand.

Advocate of Time   Craig Allan

Suddenly, Pharaoh finally realizes that Moses had told him the truth all along; that the God of Israel would not be put off or shut out. That He alone reigns over the earth and that Pharaoh himself has only been a selfish and arrogant false idol who would not willingly and honestly worship the one true God.

Pharaoh raises his arms skyward in a last effort to draw strength from his empty reign over Egypt. As he reaches skyward and screams, the sound of crushing ice and rushing water drowns out his cries. Pharaoh and his army are washed away in falling ice and water, and are lost forever. Eleven miles west on the western shore of the sea a handful of Egyptians survive the crashing waves of the returning sea. They will live to tell the triumphant tale of how God fought for the nation of Israel. How the ruler of Egypt and his fruitless armies were lost to the waters of the Red Sea in a single swipe of Gods mighty hand.

The waters of the red sea wash in quickly on the eastern shore as the Israelites rush backward to avoid being drawn in by the surf and the undertow. Moses lowers his arms and turns toward Gods people.

"This day will be remembered always as the day that God in heaven saved the nation of Israel from the wrath of Pharaoh and the army of Egypt. God be praised."

In one voice the nation of Israel shouts,

"God be praised!"

Eddie and his friends stand a ways south of the large mass of people dancing and singing their praises to God. They are in awe of the most amazing event their eyes have ever witnessed. At the edge of the crowd of people they notice a woman dancing a praising God. They immediately recognize her as the woman from the throne room of Pharaoh, the woman who was subconsciously watching them pass. She is wrapped in praise and worship.

 "Ag," Eddie shouts, "is that..?"

"Yes Eddie," he replies, "that is the pagan woman. She is now a child of God. He found her where she was, she accepted Him as the one and only true God, she has been forgiven and she has finally been set free."

 Eddie grins from ear to ear, "I'm glad we were able to see that; she looks so peaceful and happy."

They sit down together and cry for joy and for the loss of so many disobedient people. It's not an easy thing to witness God's wrath and they have experienced much of it.

Advocate of Time Craig Allan

Aganon steps toward the inland area. He looks at his charge and smiles. "You all have made me very proud to be part of something so amazing. I am honored to be called your friend."

"We are the ones who are honored Ag;" Eddie says.

They nod in agreement.

"Thanks ya'll," Aganon says with a wide and glowing smile, "Let's head inland and have a rest and then we'll make our plans on where to go from here."

"Yeah," Eddie says, "Okay."

Chapter 15

The travelers go home

Aganon and his charge sit in a tight circle reflecting on the events of the last week. In the distance they can hear the song and shouts of the nation of Israel as they sing their songs of praise. They are moving inland toward Mt. Sinai and their new home and their future.

"So what's our next move my friends?" Joey asks breaking the moment of silence.

"Up to ya'll I reckon," Aganon says with a drawl. Everyone laughs.

"This has been a wonderful and great adventure," Eddie says with wonder in his voice, "but I think it's time to go home and reflect on what we have experienced. We need some time to grow and recover. Don't you guys think so?"

"Yeah," Angela says, "I think you're right Eddie. "It's time to go home."

"Yep," Robbie says in agreement. "I could use some rest."

"So then it's decided?" Aganon asks. "Going home?"

They all look around at each other and at Aganon. They nod one at a time in agreement.

"Very well," Aganon continues, "we'll rest here today and tonight, gather our strength. Then tomorrow we'll follow along behind the Israelites and find a place to travel from."

"Sounds good to me Aggie," Becky says sounding relieved.

"I am pretty tired," Robbie adds.

"Yeah," Eddie says in agreement, "I think we all are."

They sit around a tiny fire and reflect some more about their week of travel among the nation of Egypt and the tribe of Israel. They talk about what they have learned about Moses and his life, and the great and wonderful things God has done in their past and in their lives.

Each of them naps and sleeps, they eat and pray, they reflect and share what each has received from God. As night falls they gather together around the fire and eat their diner. They finally ask Aganon questions about his life and what it must be like to be an angel. He tells them as much as he is able, but enough to satisfy their curiosity. Eventually, one at a time, they lay down to sleep. The stars wink in and out in the ancient sky above them. They sleep deeply and safely in the arms of Jesus. They feel a peace and a comfort that has never been felt by them before, maybe never again. Aganon sits beside the diminishing fire and thinks of the things in his long and distant past. This experience with these wonderful kids has awakened the sleep of time within him and brought back many memories of things gone past and things forgotten. Time passes and the sky winks and twinkles as the night passes slowly.

"Taking them home then my friend?" Percival asks from behind Aganon.

"You say true my old friend," Aganon replies without looking around, "it is time."

"I reckon so Aggie," Percival says with a wry smile as he walks around and sits by the fading fire.

"You really enjoy calling me Aggie don't you Percy?" Aganon says playfully.

"Every bit as much as you like calling me Percy old friend," Percival say with equal playfulness.

"Indeed," Aganon "I surely do my friend."

"How was it this time?" Aganon asks, knowing the answer.

"Not so bad on your group this time friend," Percival says with surprise in his voice. "More forces were spent on the events the Most High set in motion in the Sea. The battle raged with fierce and continuous waves of attack. They wanted to take down some of the Hebrews to prove a point I suppose. We were even able to save more Egyptians than we had originally planned."

"The outcome is always the same," Aganon mentions as a thought, "but this is the first time they have ever been part of it." He says wagging his head toward his sleeping young friends.

"I was not part of the battle," Percival says, "at least not in their time. Although I was there in this time fighting as a warrior, in their time I am their protector and I stood fast to look after them. The duty of my charge and all ya know." Percival says with a wink.

"Sure I know my friend," Aganon replies with a hint of laughter in his voice. "What is it they say? Been there; done that," they laugh together for a moment.

"You gonna miss them Ag?" Percival ask with no hesitation.

"Sure I will Percy," Aganon replies quickly, "I have grown quite fond of them."

"There is always a chance they will want to travel again my friend," Percival says putting his hand on Aganon's shoulder. "I'm sure they will have more questions and more desire to see things when The Almighty will allow it."

"Sure," Aganon says, "I know. They are not going to be gone from me for all time. I may see them again. I sure hope so anyway."

They look toward the brightening eastern sky as the sun prepares to rise on another day in the ancient land of the time of Israel. After a long time of silence Aganon asks another question.

"Will you continue to be the head of their guardian charge?" He asks Percival.

He does not answer.

"Percy?" Aganon turns to him and he is gone. "Ugh, he got me again."

"We'll meet again soon I'm sure my old friend," Percival says stepping up from behind Aganon. He thrusts out his hand once more.

"You'd think I'd be wise to you by now Percy," Aganon says in a playful tone of annoyance, "I'm gonna miss your sudden visits my friend," and he takes his hand. They shake fervently, and then Percival turns and strides out into the fading darkness and melts into the last bit of night.

"They are a fortunate bunch to have you as their watcher Percy," Aganon says to the shadows, "fortunate indeed."

Aganon watches the sun come up on the eastern horizon. He rebuilds the fire as his young friends begin to stir and awaken one by one. As they gather at the fire and absorb its warmth, they slowly begin to recall the events of the days past. They gather up their belongings and take care of their personal needs. Once they have all gathered back at the fire Aganon passes the pack of food around once more.

"How did everyone rest?" He asks, "Well I hope."

"It gets better each time Aggie," Becky says.

"Does it? Aganon asks. "That's good."

"Ya'll needed a good rest," He says, "yesterday was a big day."

"Sure was," Eddie adds. "I think we are all ready for today as well."

"You say true Eddie," Aganon says in agreement.

Advocate of Time   Craig Allan

"We'll set out as soon as ya'll are ready," he says.

"Sounds good," Angela says, "I could use a good long bath." They all laugh and agree that each of them could take at least a two or three hour bath.

They finish their breakfast and gather up what is left of their belongings. They all gather around Aganon to have a word of prayer. They pray for nine or ten minutes and take some time to meditate on Gods plan for their lives. When they are done they wait for Aganon's lead.
"Okay friends," Aganon says, "time to take a bit of a walk, shouldn't be too long."

"We could use a little walking after all that sleeping," Robbie adds. They laugh again.

They set out along the path of the Israelite exodus. The ground is fairly flat and desert like, and they must find a suitable fixture to use to create their last portal of this journey; the doorway home. They walk for several hours before coming across some of the remnants of the first group of Hebrews to get tired of carrying some of their belongings. Eddie finds all sorts of items that have been discarded; blankets, bowls and cups, ornaments, wood and straw bundles, things that look like they were too heavy and burdensome to carry anymore.

"There will be much more of this along the way," Aganon says.

"This is just the beginning," Eddie adds.

They continue for another two hours when they come across a rock formation that has a small tree growing out of the middle of the rocks. The tree is only a few feet taller than Aganon, but it will certainly suit their needs.

"Looks like the place," Aganon says, "anyone need to rest before we walk out?"

"Yeah," Eddie says, "let's take a few minutes before we go."

"Yeah," Angela adds, "a little breather."

"You betcha," Aganon says playfully.

They sit and rest on the rocks for twenty or thirty minutes. Then slowly they gather up around the tree. Aganon walks up to the tree as well. They look at it as if looking at a long lost friend. Finally Aganon takes out his lariat and simply tosses the loop over the top of the tree. He steps back two paces and holds the rope up to his shoulder level.

"Ready?" He asks.

"Yep," Eddie says for all of them, "I think we are ready."

"Okay," Aganon says, "let's do this."

He points to the doorway he has created and a bluish swirl begins to appear in the very middle of the squared area his rope has created against the tree and himself. The bluish swirl begins to birth deep purple highlights and then it opens in the center like and eye of a storm and grows in size as it turns and swirls. The scene they see is of the park at the end of town across the street from the Webster Study Inn. When they see it in the dark Webster night, they begin to smile in unison. It is as if they have been gone for years. The portal reaches its full size then stops its rotation and stills. They look at Aganon.

"Why did it stop turning Ag?" Angela asks.

"Yeah," Laura adds, "all the other ones continued to swirl as we went through them."

Aganon continued to look at them with awe and love. Finally Eddie speaks up.

"Because this is the final portal isn't it Ag. This is the last one, once we go through this doorway, we won't be able to travel anymore."

Advocate of Time   Craig Allan

"That is correct Eddie," Aganon replies in love, "at least not in this time sequence anyway. You are always so intuitive about these things Eddie. God's wisdom is so present in you and your friends."

"You're not coming with us," Becky says with tears in her eyes, "this is goodbye, isn't it Ag?"

"Yes Becky," Aganon replies with sadness in his voice, "this is the end of the line for me. Once you all go through there is no going back, and I will not be coming through with you."

With tears Angela asks, "But why Aggie?" with a sob breaking on her voice.

"Now don't cry little lady," Aganon drawls, "I'm sure we'll meet again someday." They laugh a little at his John Wayne drawl.

"It's not the end of your road,"Aganon adds, "or the end of mine, not even the end of our road together, just this particular stretch of road; that's all."

Eddie walks right up to Aganon and embraces him tightly.

"You have been an inspiration to us all Ag," Eddie says, his voice cracking, "I'll not forget you."

"Nor I you Edward," Aganon says, "You are a good man, and a great leader. Keep God first in all you are, and in all you do and you will achieve anything you can possibly imagine."

"Thanks Ag," Eddie says. Then in a sudden and deliberate movement he steps back from Aganon and steps right through the portal. On the other side he turns toward the portal where they can see him facing them, and he waits for his friends.

Angela steps up to Aganon and hugs him tightly.

"You are truly one of Gods greatest creatures Aganon of time," she says. "I'll never forget you."

"I'll never forget you Angela," Aganon tells her, "I almost called you Angel a few times; you have shown me what it is like to be tender and loving with one another. Something I have not experienced in a very very long time. Thank you."

"You are most welcome sir," she says and then she turns from him and steps through the portal to Eddie's side. She faces the portal and waits patiently.

Laura and Robbie step up to Aganon and they hug him together.
"Thanks Ag," Laura says, "it's been a great ride."

"It's been my pleasure Laura, you keep your chin up and your faith true, you'll be just fine."

"Thanks Ag," she says, "you too."

"I will Laura," he replies.

"I've never met an angel before Aggie," Robbie says tearfully, "but I bet you are one of the very best. I'm gonna miss you man."

"I'll miss you to Robert," he says, "keep up the fight my friend. You are more than conquerors you know."

"Yep," Robbie says, "we'll see ya." They step away from Aganon and walk through together and stand with their friends on the other side.

Joey and Becky step up to Aganon; Joey hugs him. Becky waits behind him.
"Will we ever see you again Ag?" He asks.

"Of course Joseph," he says, "one day we will meet again. I'm certain of it."

"Okay," Joey says with tears in his eyes, "catch ya later buddy." He turns from Aganon, looks at Becky. He wipes his eyes and walks through the portal to stand with Eddie and the others.

Becky is left standing alone with Aganon. She runs to him and embraces him tightly. She holds him for awhile then looks up into his loving, shining face.

"I am still not sure if we are all dreaming or if this is actually real Ag. I have seen and heard so much. I'm not sure if I'll be able to make any sense of it all."

"You will Rebecca," Aganon says to her with love, "I promise you; you will."

"It is a lot for now, but if God was not certain you could bear it, he would not have sent you along." He says to her with comfort in his voice.

"I guess you're right Ag," She says. "I guess I better go, the others are standing there waiting."

"Yeah," he says, "you probably should."

"You really are a beautiful person Aggie," she says lovingly squeezing him one more time.

"And so are you Rebecca," he says, "a most beautiful person indeed."

She finally breaks her embrace of him. She steps back and looks at him one more time in his cowpoke clothes and his large brimmed hat.

"You really are a sight my friend," she says with a laugh. Then she steps through the portal. She turns to face him and they all stand and stare back at their new, old friend. He nods to them and they nod in return. They turn and make their way to their cars parked out front of the Webster Study Inn. It is 8:11 pm on the same night they left. Becky looks back at the portal one last time and waves again to Aganon. He waves back and then she turns and walks with her friends into their new future and their new relationship with their Great God. They have so much more to learn about the things they have seen. But they have the necessary tools to make their way through the truth, and to find the knowledge in the written word of God. Theirs is a journey and adventure in the beginning.

Aganon watches them fade into the dark night of Webster. He feels a slight pang of despair for the times they shared together and the time alone he will spend without them. Yet, he knows there are other places and other travelers. His time will not be spent alone. He draws the rope upward and off the tree and the portal remains. He rolls up the rope and stows it into his coat again. He crouches down and leaps into the air. He instantly takes flight into the bright sky of ancient Arabia. As he ascends, his cowpoke clothing vanishes in light and color and returns to his angelic cover. He then begins to turn and descend in full glory back to the ground. In the distance to the south he sees the progression of the nation of Israel making their way to Jebel El Lawz also known as Mt. Sinai. He descends faster and faster back to earth as his shining light brightens and flows. He looks back toward the sea; he sees the specks of the fallen army of Egypt on the shores. Such loss for such an easy and simple gift, God gives life freely; all they have to do is accept it. Few do, so many are lost that need not be. He is happy to have met six that have taken the gift and will do so much with it. Many more will come to the cross of Christ, yet, so many more need to be shown. His job is to make time for them to come, too raise those who will bring the message of hope to the lost. So much to do, he must not waste time.

He descends out of the sky like a comet falling to earth. He approaches the ground in a streak; just before he hits the ground he pulls up swiftly and shoots through his portal like a bullet. The portal explodes in a flash of lightning and waves of light. The air around ripples briefly then settles. The dust falls and settles as well. At the bottom of the cluster of rocks, Percival, angel of the watch, observes as his friend returns to receive his command.
"Show off," he says to the bright day.

He walks up the hill to the twinkling specks that remain of the portal and walks through and he is gone. He has returned to his charge in Webster. The floating lights and specs of shiny dust fade out. The air is still and nothing moves. Twenty miles southeast the nation of Israel are about to begin their new life. They glorify God and sing His praises; For He is mighty and able to deliver his faithful unto salvation.

Where will Aganon the Angel of time go next? Don't miss out on the next biblical adventure with Aganon in Advocate of Time: The Becoming.

David walks through the heavily wooded forest looking for a missing lamb. While he was leading the flock toward the valley bottom a straggler was taken.

"Lord, I know this baby has been taken, I found the track of a robust bear and the wool pulled from the coat. Oh Lord, permit me to strike the bear down and recover our precious lamb. I am not afraid Lord. Strengthen my hand and my staff to do battle for Your honor."

As the young shepherd slowly and prayerfully tracks through trees, following the tracks of the bear he hears the lamb's cries off in the distance, he stops abruptly to listen. He swiftly turns to his left and silently lunges through the underbrush toward the sound of the frightened lamb. He closes in on the sound of the bear lumbering through the short grass with the lamb caught firmly in his powerful jaws. As the bear rounds a large evergreen tree David lunges out from behind it, startling the bear, causing him to drop the lamb. The lamb scurries behind David and he takes a defensive stance facing the bear.

Aganon walks swiftly through the trees looking back on occasion to wave the others onward. As Aganon crests the small rise of a hill he stops suddenly and crouches in the grass. Eddie and his friends come up alongside Aganon and look in the direction he is looking. In the trees about twenty yards away is a very young man in shepherds clothing hiding behind a large tree. Aganon points to the left of the young man toward a small meadow of short grass as a large black bear lumbers out of the brush with a white mass hanging from his mouth. It's a lamb, taken from this young man's flock.

"It's David!" Angela shrieks.

David suddenly glances in the direction of Aganon and his charge. They all duck down with exception of Aganon who stands his ground.

"Oh Lord," Angela sighs, "Did he hear me Aggie?"

"Of course not Angela," Aganon assures her, "he heard something, probably certain of a bird, see, he's already looking back at the bear coming his way."

Angela looks back the way Aganon is pointing and sees David sizing up his situation. The shepherd boy crouches slightly with his staff raised and poised for action. As the bear approaches his hiding place he leaps out and startles the bear. The bear drops the lamb and it scurries to safety behind David. The bear roars violently at David and tries to lunge around him to recapture his prey but David side-steps the bear's movement and blocks him. The bear now irritated stands up on its hind legs. This makes him at least a foot taller than David and much wider. The bear assumes the boy will flee, he does not. The bear swings his massive paw toward David in an attempt to scare him away; David continues to stand his ground. Frustrated by the courageous display by this annoying human the bear drops down to his legs and lunges toward David in an attempt to knock David to the ground. The bears head is lowered as he charges and David anticipated this attack and side steps the bear swiftly, delivering a crushing blow with his staff to the bear's huge head just behind its ear. The sound of the blow echoes through the woods like a gunshot, the spectators flinch in surprise at the sharp sound.

"Oh man," Eddie winces, "that had to hurt."

As the bear reels and rocks back from the swift blow he spends a split second on his decision to continue the attack or retreat, the bear is hungry and makes the wrong choice. He swiftly swivels toward David, rearing up in a foolish attempt to capture David with his massive paws and draw him in to his waiting maw. David sees it coming and reaches out with his strong left hand, grasps the hide under the chin of the bear with one fluid motion. Before the creature can react with its powerful jaws David brings down the full force of his staff across the eyes of the black bear. The sound of crushing bone and breaking skull is sharp and final. The bear is knocked to the ground immediately and before its shattered mind can register what has happened David's knife is on its throat. Its life blood spills onto the forest floor. The battle is over and David's faith has delivered him again. He stands over the bear breathing slowly, steadily. Looking sympathetically at the dying black beast he kneels down and touches the bear on its shoulder, comforting the animal until it has breathed its last. He was a worthy adversary. He stows his knife, says a prayer of praise to Jehovah and scoops up the lamb, slinging the relieved baby around his neck he strides off toward the valley where the flock is waiting.

Aganon and his charge stand amazed, watching the young warrior king walk out of sight into the heavily wooded forest, toward his own charge.

"I'm in amazement," Robbie bursts out, breaking the silence and startling the others.

"Good night Robbie," Angela scolds swatting in his direction, "that scared me."

"That was pretty awesome guys," he says with excitement "what a fierce and amazing battle."

"He fought for The Lord, with the strength and power of Jehovah," Aganon replies.

"I'll say," Joey adds, "I've never seen anything like that."

"Yeah," Becky confirms, "but you will again. It was so amazing how he helped that poor animal along in its death. He actually had compassion on the bear, but it's certain the bear would have killed him and probably eaten him."

"Yep," Eddie agrees," that's our David, future king of Israel."

"What an amazing man," Laura sighs, "sure would be something to know him."

"Sure would," Eddie agrees, "where to next? We have much more to see."
"He's right y'all," Aganon agrees, "where to now?"

Robbie suggests, "How, about a word of prayer?"

"Indeed," Aganon agrees.

"A valiant idea Robbie," Eddie delights, "will you lead us Robbie?"

"Absolutely, join us Aggie?"

The closely knit group of time travelers huddles into a circle and Robbie reaches his hand to Aganon. He smiles brightly, takes Robbie's offering joins hands with Becky and looks heavenward. They observe his delight and do likewise. Robbie leads in a fervent prayer of thanksgiving, joy, faithfulness and resounding intercession as he prays for his friends and their future together, both in this ancient land and time to come.

David comes into view of his flock and stops just inside the tree line of the forest. His little one is resting comfortably in his arms now, emotionally shaken but has calmed since he left the bear behind.

"That was quite an adventure little one," he says gently, rubbing her neck lovingly.

"Back to mama and papa now," he steps into the opening of the valley and the nearest sheep in the fold look up at him. Two adult sheep cry out toward him and turn. The little one in his arms begins to come alive and wiggle, hearing her parent's voices. David puts her gently on the ground and rubs her neck one more time. As he straightens she bolts off toward the flock and her waiting parents. He watches the reunion and feels a sense of fulfillment and completion. He is happy, content and ready to face the next adventure. Little does he know his life is about to be transformed forever.

Coming soon.

Advocate of Time
The Becoming
By
Craig Allan

www.ingramcontent.com/pod-product-compliance
Lightning Source LLC
Chambersburg PA
CBHW051432170626
46809CB00006B/2427